# The Heretic Emperor

# CONTENTS

## PREFACE

To penetrate the mystery that was Maximillian Scarlotti, we have been forced to draw testimony from a wide disharmony of sources. After absorbing these discrepit portrayals, the reader will be better positioned to understand how disaster unfolded. Those who have ears, let them hear.

For we *Weltverbesserer* (or 'globalists' as our enemies like to call us) the lesson must be learnt and learnt well if our project is to blossom again, no matter in what far future. For although we lost a mighty battle, the war goes on and on.

Even so, two things have of late changed the battlefield beyond recognition, the first being the Grey Death. The other, of course, was the strange life of our even stranger adversary, Maxi Scarlotti – the one who managed to pull the rug from under us when we were in a seemingly unassailable position – something that must never be allowed to happen again.

The most revealing statement we possess from the hand of Maxi himself is a written testimony from his early years – the first document presented in this portfolio. From thence, other voices will take up the tale.

- Elmer J. Cohen
(former) Special Advisor to the
(former) Unicursal Curia

1

## THE TESTIMONY OF
## MAXIMILLIAN SCARLOTTI

I am leaving tomorrow, so I wish to put my thoughts in order. It seems to start with the dream. While I have had many recurring dreams since early childhood (like that of the empty Sears building in Chicago full of cobwebs in the moonlight, now a dangerous wreck), the one that came to me three times of late at Sterns is markedly different, due chiefly to its visceral intensity. On waking each time, I *felt* the strips of flesh under my fingernails – my own flesh.

*In this dream I am a child of six or seven, but strong, almost as strong as a man already. And I am springing at a warrior twice my height – a tall German.*

*I am leaping, attempting to kill him. The scene is a castle where he has imprisoned me, and while the prison is a luxurious one, I hate him for it. I try to tear his flesh, but he beats me off with ease – so I turn on myself, ripping at clothes and skin with sharp little fingernails, gouging red and jagged stripes into my chest. Some of the onlookers are shocked, but for others it merely confirms the rumours, for it is whispered that I am the son of a butcher or a demon…that my birth was public, like that of Antichrist. Some say I* am *the Antichrist, but I don't believe it.*

*Then, I somehow* know *that later the same year this tall warrior will already be gone to his long home – cut down at a place where Hannibal once decimated the armies of Rome many centuries ago. For some reason, this strikes me as profoundly significant.*

*Then I awake, clawing at my chest. I feel the deep gouges in my flesh, but this is illusory, as my nails are perfectly blunt.*

It was this *dream* that first encouraged me to explore outside the confines of Sterns, making a solo voyage into the African darkness that is darker yet by day. There had been nothing technically impeding me from doing so, for at Sterns, a blind eye is traditionally turned to students who feel the urge to sneak out on surreptitious weekend missions, taking only a handgun for protection, in order to observe what the school authorities call 'unredeemed humanity' – Homo sapiens bereft of the blessings of the World State – but it had never interested me before; so here I was, doing it for the first time, two months before graduation.

The nearby market town, Masongo, is the centre of a lively region near the the edge of the Kenyan highlands. Despite the thin air, a thick and macabre menace permeates the atmosphere of the town, rolling down its grenadine, garbage-strewn streets, and forming a sinister cloud in the centre – the marketplace, scene of violence as often as commerce.

On the occasion of my first visit I was witness to the spectacle of a small truck, creaking as it wobbled beneath an enormous pile of garbage, crashing, as if in slow motion, into a tree stump on which stood a hatchet-faced baboon.

The chained yellow monkey, buried under such a vast tract of refuse, could scarcely have survived – it must surely have suffocated under the avalanche of filthy plastic bags in the time that its owner spent screeching and booming at the truck driver, while his woman looked on from across her ugali pot.

Then, two mottled black urchins attempted to pick my pockets as I watched the conflict unfold and almost made away with my precious handgun...and while fending them off, I noticed something damnedly strange: a white man was staring at me. An old white man with a long beard, who clearly had nothing to do with Sterns. Indeed, his steely blue-grey eyes were like nothing I had seen on this planet before, and I couldn't meet that winnowing glance for long…

But when I looked again, he was gone.

Then a brawl flared out across the marketplace, and a lynch mob began to coalesce, with the aim of stringing up the hapless baboon-killer, so I left the stench of 'unredeemed humanity' for the more civilised surroundings of Sterns.

On returning, after the usual infection check pertaining to such expeditions, I headed to the television room to unwind. A spell of passive voyeurism would soon help me to forget the *real* Africa.

And there, just outside the door, standing with folded arms, was Tegg. A quiet, dreamlike girl so utterly different from the other students that I still have no idea how on earth she ended up there. In the nearly two years since our mutual arrival at Sterns, I had scarcely given a thought to her sweetly freckled face (like that of a highly intelligent yet timid marsupial mouse), but now something happened – she *looked* at me. It was a look that signified something, I knew not what…which made it the second significant glance I had received that day.

I smiled frigidly back, not wanting to betray the sudden upsurge of feeling in its pristine private nest (where I naturally expected it would stay), and she bit her lip as if working up the courage to speak – but as I couldn't bring myself to slow my steps (O utter fool!) and, as no speech was forthcoming, my locomotion carried me cruelly onwards, into the darkened opium den of the television chamber, where a dozen students stared fascinated at the news, which showed footage of mass demonstrations now taking place across Europe.

"Fresh protests yesterday against the Archetype in Hannover and in Mainz," intoned the reader, over footage of frenzied parades where dreadlocked Antifa mixed with sharply dressed yuppie careerists, all of them screeching *"Smash the Archetype! Smash the Archetype!"*

The kids in the TV room were grinning excitedly and saying "This is *our* work!", high-fiving each other and so forth. And I should have been part of it too, but something in me felt cold. I returned to the corridor...but Tegg had gone. In her place, now walking rapidly towards me, was Tricia Philips, my affianced. Normally Tricia's perfect, blandly symmetrical face would have put my doubts at ease, but today it had the opposite effect, thrusting my nerves into overdrive. It felt as if her visage was sucking out all my remaining calm and using it to feather her own enervation – just a cosmetic layer, of course, as there wasn't a bone of doubt in her.

"Hey, the sex room's free if you want to," she breathed, with a half-smothered yawn. At eighteen, sex had already become something mechanical and joyless for her.

The sex room at Sterns is a sterile, comfortable chamber with controlled lighting, filled with various dispensers of prophylactic and lubricatory substances, birth control manuals (as if we could forgot the constant lectures!) and so forth. Senior students, even faggots, are encouraged to form heterosexual 'partnerships' to further their career ambitions among the unenlightened – nothing to do with love, of course (not that love is forbidden, just no one at Sterns believes in it).

Anyhow, Tricia is something of a traditionalist, that is to say, one who favours retaining the *form* of open marriage for strategic reasons – as against the faction who think its usefulness is played out. But the thought of her lying naked on a rubber-coated mattress beneath the Warmth Lanterns, her genitals coated in some sterile, factory-flavoured substance, making small talk about our upcoming final exams as I tupped her, filled me with a vicious sunburst of claustrophobic quease.

"I'm not in the mood," I stammered.

"That's fine, Maxi," she said. "Maybe later…or we could listen to the Storyteller instead."

"Okay," I agreed, relieved. It wasn't like Tricia to suggest the Storyteller, who held court here of Sundays like a blind poet of yore (not that he actually *was* blind, but he gave that impression for some reason)…in fact she had never shown the slightest bit of interest in him before, but end-of-year madness was upon us all it seemed, even stolid Tricia. And as we were walking down the corridor holding formulaic hands, she asked what I had been up to.

"I went out into Africa, alone," I murmured.

"Oh, wow. I still remember the time *I* went. Late last year, with Seth and Jemma. It *stank*. Never again! Interesting place, though."

Tricia and I had been an 'item' since January, and indeed, as star pupils of our year it had always been more or less expected that we would form an 'alliance with benefits', so to speak, and that we were destined for big things – but now, as we entered the Storyteller's chamber, I suddenly felt very small and uncertain.

The talker was there, telling his audience of three (now five) a horror story – at least that's what I think it was supposed to be. His dark eyes sparkled in the glow of the brazier as we sat in the silken darkness listening to his recitation of an epic about the war and suffering caused by 'Kshatriyan aristocrats', who as our teachers never ceased to remind us brutally governed the world in days gone by, and "that's why we're in the mess we're in now," etc. etc. But the Kshatriyas weren't wrong to want order, they assured us – it was simply the wrong *kind* of order. They were an elite who brought suffering as well as greatness.

"Our goal is a world completely *devoid* of suffering,"

the Storyteller reminded us.

"But why, then," spoke a voice from the shadows, "does Mr. Snow *[The PE and martial arts teacher at Sterns – E.J.C.]* make us *suffer* so?" There were chortles. The voice belonged to Bryn, something of a class clown. Back in first year, he had been considered somewhat suspect due to his obsession with Hermann Hesse's 'glass bead game' – something he vocally intended recreating. Hesse, of course, is now seen as a 'proto-fascist' (despite his pacifist beliefs) by dominant taste setters.

But the teachers must have seen *something* in Bryn, for they kept him at the school despite his raving. And their foresight proved correct, for in second year Bryn had become considerably more orthodox. Now the other students could relax and laugh at his jokes, because he no longer mentioned the insufferable German romantic. And the Storyteller, too, politely chuckled at Bryn's remark.

"Mr. Snow teaches you pain," he said, "so that others won't be able to. We must be *strong* if we are to eliminate strength, and suffering along with it…"

And so here it was that my own thoughts began to coalesce.

I was already beginning to feel that, at Sterns, the atmosphere of an idealist project was a superficial one. Not only that, but deep down I was beginning to sense it was the *wrong* idealist project.

\*   \*   \*

Next Saturday, I went back to the township. All was as before, and the mess was such that you couldn't tell there had been a riot and a lynching. To my surprise, a strange black *gamin fée* approached and beckoned me to follow him: "Mistah Kurtz, he want see you now," he whispered, and I laughed out loud in spite of myself.

I followed him on what turned out to be a ten mile trek through the countryside. There were no adventures on the way, despite my apprehension of lions…or worse, an armed gang of the kind that occasionally raided from across the Somalian border. There were only the vultures, staring mournfully from baobab trees…and then when we finally turned off the dusty track, walking across grasslands for the final mile, a serval cat grinning at us from its shelter in a hollow log. Then night emerged, swiftly and brutally, all becoming a blur except for the cave ahead, a silver spray of glowworms irradiating its mouth in the thickening dark. I shuddered, wondering if the old man was home (for I had known from the first, of course, where I was going). The *gamin* turned away, plodding emotionlessly back the way he'd come, and so I stood alone before the dark gate to mystery. Two Anglo-Nubian goats paced impassively in a nearby enclosure – the old man's source of milk, no doubt. How did he guard them from predators, I wondered idly.

"Well, are you coming in or not?" The deep-crusted English-accented voice boomed out at me from another plane of being. I shivered and made my way into the cave, ducking to avoid the hanging rock at the entrance. His eyes were glittering in the near-dark of the atrium, lit only by a flickering glow from a chamber further back. Into the latter he led me, and we sat before an open fire in the middle of the craggy cavern. The cave smoked, although a chimney hole of sorts in the roof provided minimal ventilation.

"I won't beat around the bush," he growled. "I have a gift for sensing past lives of others. And as I was wandering the world, rather close to one of those indoctrination centres where future evil is trained and directed, I suddenly sensed the presence of *greatness*. Of a powerful spirit from the past. I don't know *which* spirit, but a great one. And so I nested in the area, hoping for this reincarnation to show itself. And when I saw you in the market, I instantly knew it was you. So overwhelmed was I by the feeling of world-historical greatness that I withdrew in shock.

"But it didn't take me long to recover my senses, after which I set a few of the local urchins to watch for your reappearance…for, with my persona, it was easy to make them fear me, the powerful 'white warlock', and they obeyed on pain of death. They think nothing of a ten mile trek through the bush, either. I could sense your presence for nearly half an hour before you finally arrived, you know."

I was taken aback at all this, yet unsurprised. *There were the dreams.* But I said nothing of these. Instead, I asked what he actually wanted, and he calmly smiled.

"To set you on the right track. To free you from the grip of evil. I know all about that *institution* you're embroiled at." Rapidly, with hypnotic voice, he began to expound his doctrine of *esoteric ethnopluralism*, talking of fractals, of hundred-armed swastikas and thousand-branched candelabras.

And I listened in the glow of the moth-spangled firelight, taking it all in. I will remember it until my dying day.

"Evolution springs from a silent centre," he intoned. "From the unconscious of God. It is the duty of our Order to help that centre grow into a multifacteted labyrinth."

In spite of myself, I was thrilled that he had said *our* Order…that *I* was included in such a grand and secretive project. Enrollment at Sterns was supposed to make me part of an elite, but it had always felt hollow – and here, now, finally, was a *real* elite, one I could be proud to fight for…no matter that no normal person, when gazing on my corpse, would even know I had belonged to it!

"And so, needless to say," he continued, "for those of us who want to *increase* the diversity in the universe, the doctrine of globalism is anathema, the ultimate evil. The multicultural 'melting pot' destroys the earth's myriad of unique cultures by depriving them of authority, assimilating them to the global fast-food anti-culture..."

I had heard this argument before, of course, from a member of the cult known as Wolves of Joy (I think everyone now knows of *them*), and had dismissed it with a counterargument of my own. But somehow it was different hearing it in a firelit cave in the African bush, with the mad laughter of hyenas in the background like nocturnal spirits of unrest.

Nevertheless, determined to show the old man that I had thrown in my lot with the Sterns globalists for entirely *honourable* reasons, I reiterated the counterargument forcefully…

"If you give authority to *all* the 'unique cultures'," I said, "it will result in war and suffering, and then in the smaller cultures being swallowed by more powerful or persuasive ones, until few, or only *one* are left. Thus, globalism is inevitable, and so we should we seek to attain it by the shortest possible path, the way of *least* suffering, rather than that of war, conflicting nationalisms, regionalisms, tribalisms and so forth."

"I anticipated you would say so," he smiled. "For that is what your Jewish teachers at Sterns have taught you to…"

"Not *all* of them are Jews," I interjected angrily.

"No, not all of them, to be sure. I believe at least one of them isn't. And I'm impressed enough by their argument to expound to you, right here and now, the second and more esoteric doctrine of our Order. The doctrine of *Imperium*."

"What's that?"

"I mean that the periphery cannot hold without a strong centre whose force guards and protects the many-faceted paths."

"You mean a kind of globalist anti-globalism? With a central body at the top?"

"With a *single* body at the top – an emperor, Imperator."

"But who's to say he won't become corrupt, and bring in the melting pot anyway, with greater force than even the Unicursal Curia would be able to?"

"That is why he must be a *man*, not a council or committee. Because a man with the right training can keep himself pure, whereas a council cannot."

"And how on earth do you propose to get this hypothetical princeps to attain power in the first place, let alone keep it?"

He smiled again.

"I already said that I sense greatness in you, and can help to bring it out. The rest is up to you."

I shuddered violently at the enormity of what he was saying.

At dawn, he led me outside to see the Morning Star.

"Our sign," he said, bowing his head in reverence. "The symbol of our Order."

As if by some illusion, that cold sigil now seemed more remote than the fixed stars themselves, and an indescribable loneliness stabbed me in the guts.

"Please, let this cup pass from me," I murmured, but the Morning Star said nothing in response.

\*    \*    \*

The first person I saw on my return was Tegg, who

was waiting by the school gate as if looking out for me. In fact, she *was* looking out for me, and when sighted, it seemed as if she was struggling with herself.

"So *there* you are," she stuttered. "You know, they're already talking about sending search parties out. You'd better report to the director's office at once."

The freckles on her face were like the stars of the Milky Way, scattering my heart to the far void…such cream of sweetness, such aching melancholy. I knew now it was the face of my astral beloved, *but how had I failed to recognise her before?* Surely I must pay for this transgression…

There was an unspoken bond between us, and I wondered if she, like me, bore the mark of Cain. So I asked her outright:

"Do you ever have strange rememberances?"

"What do you mean?"

"Dreams you were once…someone else."

"Like reincarnation?"

"Call it that if you want."

"I'm not sure. If I *have* lived before then I'm not sure if I'd *want* to know."

"Why not?"

She paused and considered a moment before replying.

"Do you remember Kyle?"

"Hopkins, who got expelled in first year?"

"Yes. Well, he claimed he was pursuing a philosophy of total awareness. Total consciousness at all times…or something like that."

"I remember now. He said it was compatible with the teachings of the school, but they didn't believe him…and perhaps it wasn't."

"Yeah, perhaps…but what I mean is, I'm not sure if I would *want* to have total awareness…as there's no light without shadows…" Her face, half-shaded as she said it,

17

was like a drawing from five hundred years ago, an etching from one of the masters beyond time.

Then our conversation was interrupted by the arrival of several teachers, and I was summoned to the director's office for an explanation of my night out of bounds. So I made up a lie about spending the night with a disgusting black prostitute, which they thankfully accepted, officially admonishing me not to do so again.

Good…they believed my mission was merely one of cavorting with 'dark and comely maidens', and so (after an additional check-up for venereal diseases) it was back to the usual routine, only waiting for a chance to speak with Tegg again.

I was disappointed, however. She didn't show her face in coming days, not even in the classes we shared. I found myself worrying she might be ill, but was unable to bring myself to mention her name aloud, or enquire about her to anyone. It was a long week, long and cruel.

\*     \*     \*

Kyle Hopkins and Bryn Sturgess were certainly not the only ones to have come under suspicion of harbouring unorthodox beliefs during my time at Sterns. Even a prominent teacher had once been relieved of his post after it had been revealed he was secretly a worshipper of Cthulhu, and working with the globalists because he thought it the best means of setting Cthulhu free. (But was he kicked out because he was wrong, or just honest? These kinds of ambiguities have contributed to my growing distrust of the Sterns brand of esotericism…no such haziness surrounds the clear and manly doctine of Esoteric Ethnopluralist Imperium!)

As I write, my mind flashes back to my own Idealism

Test, administered days before my sixteenth birthday, the final hurdle before gaining entry to the most elite school in the world. I clearly remember the examiners stressing to me as stringently as possible that true Illuminism was something far beyond the ludicrous 'clocks forward' mentality of the Skull and Bones Society, the latter being an item of priceless comedy for the staff and students of Sterns. *[The Skull and Bones, famous yet secretive fraternity of Yale University, allegedly have their clocks set forward as a sign that they are above the common herd of humanity. – E.J.C.]*

Even more did we chortle at Ellison Plugg, that chubby and drug-crazed American preacher who attained to stellar heights of fame by making wildly exaggerated claims about the Unicursal Curia. His bellicose claims that a chemically sedated and microchipped populace is both the aim of the Curia and its means of attaining power were always good for a laugh, made all the funnier because, while the spittle flies from his mouth and while he screeches and fulminates, he remains blissfully unaware that the Curia are the ones lining his pockets via sponsorship deals, and misdirecting him to describe them as a 'German Illuminati Death Cult'. We know in practice, of course, that such drugging and microchipping would be too difficult logistically, even if desirable – which it *isn't*, as it would make for subjects who couldn't appreciate the high wisdom of their rulers.

But in some ways, I have come to realise, the attitude at Sterns *is* like the 'clocks forward' mentality they claim to revile, just more subtly rendered. For while claiming to be world improvers who care boundlessly for humanity, at bottom I believe they still *see* the latter as cattle…and that's not how I see it at all, for *who would want to live in a world of cattle?*

In the week after my conversation with Tegg, I had a very memorable class with Professor Levin, in which these hints and suspicions suddenly coalesced into total conviction.

Levin is a man who tries very valiantly to get his students on side, but only partially succeeds; that is to say, his attempts to come across as foppishly self-mocking may appeal to some, but leave others with a faint feeling of disgust. Levin makes constant snide remarks about his fellow Jews, as if trying to convey that he is not as heavy-handed as some of his compatriots. This had unforeseen consequences, however, during the lesson in question, when some remark of his (giving some of his students the feeling that Jews were no longer a *completely* taboo topic for open enquiry) led to a heated Q and A session on why the student body of an apparently globalist institution like Sterns was so overwhelmingly white, with mainly Jews for professors.

"Why are there so many Jewish teachers here, but no Jewish students?" someone asked. I noticed Levin's forehead covered with tiny beads of sweat – either the question *was* unwelcome, or he had now arrived at a foreseen but important hurdle in the course of the curriculum. Either way, he tried to make the best of it. He began with a humorous anecdote ridiculing British Israelites and Black Hebrew Israelites. *[These are movements who claim that white and black people respectively are the 'true Jews', while the Jews themselves are 'Satanic imposters'. – E.J.C.]*

"You know, with the information at their disposal, you'd think these people could take the time to actually *read* the Old Testament, particularly the Book of Esther, and find irrefutable proof that the Jews of today are one and the same as those of the Book," he chuckled.

"But what has that to do with Sterns?"

"Everything," he said mysteriously, and launched into a lengthy tirade about the current strategy of the Curia and its feeder institutions such as Sterns. There was an ongoing conflict between two parties (those of us who had already heard rumours of this felt an almost sexual thrill on hearing it expounded explicitly for the first time).

One party, the Wobblers, believe that it is crucial to steep the Western world in a cultural atmosphere of 'no rules'…so that there can consequently be *no rebels*.

The other group, the Blades, oppose this, because it means the only rebels will be those who advocate *rules* (i.e. fascists, and others who believe in any kind of irrational national structure). For this reason, they want to retain 'structure' but keep the rebels harnessed solidly to the outlook of the 1968 generation. The difficulty in this, of course, is that it is now almost impossible to convince the average person that 68er ideals aren't the status quo – for indeed they are, and this explains the rise of the Wolves of Joy and similar groups.

The professor then revealed that he, and most of the other teachers at Sterns, are in the Blades camp, and the Curia as a whole is also leaning in that direction, chiefly due to the dangers inherent in the Wobbler approach.

"But the Blade strategy means we need idealists to carry our work forward. And you guys were picked *precisely* because of your idealism. I can't emphasise it strongly enough. My Jewish brethen can talk all they like about *tikkun olam*, but when it comes down to it, white people (and maybe a few East Asians) make the greatest idealists. So here we are, harnessing that idealism in the service of goals worth achiving." He rubbed his hands together, and cackled self-deprecatingly.

It was difficult to know if he was insulting his 'brethren' and complimenting us, or the other way round. There was often a strong ambiguity about the way he talked. Nevertheless, he had explained the absence of Jews in the student body to the satisfaction of most of my peers. Only Bryn looked a bit sceptical…maybe he was having a reversion.

As for myself, I was seething with disgust.

*     *     *

I made my second trip to the Old Man's cave that weekend, leaving in the early morning so as to return before nightfall. It was important not to arouse any further suspicion.

The Meister was in a pensive state, but pulled himself out of it, seemingly as eager to teach as I was eager to learn. He lapsed back into deep thought, however, when I told him of Levin's conversation. After lengthy silence, he observed that it would be far more worrying if the Wobblers were to gain ascendency.

"A world without possibility of rebellion would be far more dangerous than one in which the opposition is phoney," he pronounced, "So the Blades have effectively sealed their own doom. No matter how many idealists they enlist, the Curia will find it impossible to convince young people that globalism is anywise edgy or rebellious. We've already seen how fast the Wolves of Joy have grown in the past decade. All we have to do is take their immature rebellion, and transmute it into an Imperium. An alchemic act, for which the strictest spiritual discipline is of the utmost."

He then taught me a set of spiritual exercises, which I won't divulge here, but which have given me the great reserves of strength I will surely need for the task ahead.

The afternoon wore on, and I took my leave of the Maestro, raising my hand in salute as I left.

"Remember the Morning Star," he enjoined.

But I didn't tell him about Tegg, whose face was the starry void itself.

*   *   *

These exercises, which I had only just begun to practice, soon helped me to pass my end of year exams with unheard of brilliance – perfect marks in *every* subject. And not just perfect – I demonstrated political, administrative and military strategic skills of the highest order, giving wonder to those who had set the very questions. I plumbed the depths of scenarios they hadn't even dreamed of. Nothing like it had ever happened in the ten year history of Sterns, nor ever will again. Although I was already the best pupil in my year, this was something altogether unexpected.

One teacher wanted to retest me. The others declined, but only after lengthy interviews and discussions in which they probed my sudden über-brilliance, satisfying themselves that it wasn't ephemeral. And it wasn't, for the Old Man's exercises allowed me to tap into deep wells of the unconscious.

"The Caesars were said to have matured early," muttered one professor, scratching his wizened head in confusion.

I had a robotic 'celebration fuck' with Tricia, already sensing that I had earned her lifelong emnity for outperforming her so overwhelmingly in the exams, but it wasn't something I gave much thought to.

And then came the most incredible news of all. The Praesidium, created to replace the old EU by the Unicursal Curia (itself, of course, having replaced the old UN after the latter had become too hostile to the land of the Dead Sea), was now looking for a new and *youthful* figurehead to give it renewed propaganda appeal in a world where the Wolves of Joy are a serious spiritual force. And in light of my stunning results, would I take the job?

Again, this was something unheard of in the history of globalism. For an eighteen year old boy to be chosen as Executive Commissioner of a major world body…

"I'll be a politically active EC," I warned them (don't say that I didn't!), "and certainly don't intend to sit on my backside."

"That's fine," chortled the representative. "We know your values are sound. If you can't trust a Sternsman, who *can* you trust?"

And so it was decided. The Morning Star moves in mysterious ways.

\*   \*   \*

Who giveth with one hand, taketh away with the other one, however. It was only the next day that I learnt of Tegg's suicide. She left no note, nothing.

Her body was flown back to England before I even heard the news. It is still a wondrous mystery to me. The other students, having barely spoken to her, scarcely reacted, other than with a faint contempt for an ill-timed act that soured the mirth of graduation (and infinitely deepened the gulf between them and me). My journey to the obscure side was now complete.

The deep shock brought on an illness which lasted a week, of which I have no memory, and when I recovered it was like the rebirth of spring…my beloved's face was now emblazoned on my *inner* being, my true being. And that's where it will stay. She is more real now than she was in life. There is no more grief, no more tears. I fight for *her*.

It only remains to mention my return to the Old Man's cave for advice…it was empty, of course, there being no trace he had ever lived there, or even existed at all.

And now I realise for the first time that, in material terms, I am completely and utterly alone. So I offer a prayer to the Morning Star, whose light now illuminates the astral face of my beloved, and go on my way. Tomorrow, my new posting in Europe begins.

*I will go.*

*And see.*

*And conquer.*

And may this record stand witness as to the seriousness of my endeavour, to be made public only in the event of my death.

: Maximillian Scarlotti : Dawn :

## 2

## THE TESTIMONY OF
## KARINA SEDLÁKOVÁ

My first impressions of my boss were that a new sun had risen in the sky, wearing a subtle and slender mask of gold, and had descended to bless and protect me. I had always waited for this.

My mother told me from the earliest I can remember to "never trust a man," and although over time I came to hate my mother, this piece of advice stayed with me for the most part, against my better wishes – for, unlike her, who was beaten regularly by my Communist tyrant of a father (so she said) before he finally left when I was a baby, I am not actually *afraid* of men, and never have been. No, it is my own sex I fear, with its vague mushiness, never quite gelling with the bright-clear golden image of God I have in my head, and which I was never taught.

I don't fear men – I understand them. But I don't trust them, either, because that which I *understand* is not in keeping with the bright golden head of God either, which *dazzles* and is inscrutable.

The Chief is in keeping with it, though.

I fell in love with him from the first moment he walked into the room. Despite the fact that he was eight years younger than me, I knew him instantly as my Lord and Master – also, that I could never say so out loud, or he might vanish.

"So you're my appointed PA," he smiled, and bright

rays of purifying light filled the labyrinthine crevices of my heart. Weeks earlier I had received word of winning the position as his PA…and he was, of course, the talk of Prague. For years the public in many countries have been moody and rebellious; not just the Wolves of Joy (yes, they exist in our country as in others) but also vast brigades of internet trolls taught the public to see that everything is moribund: the Curia, the Praesidium, even Capitalism itself.

And perhaps it *is* moribund. I don't know, as politics is not my strong point. I am good at observing the politics of others, however – as that is their 'idea', just as my idea is the Golden Head of God. And as my aim is the intensification of my idea, so too is theirs, perhaps, in their own manner – and it didn't take a genius to sense the heavy air, crackling with discontent.

So Maximillian Scarlotti was installed as Executive Commissioner of the Praesidium, to give a sense that youth was in the ascendency. There was now talk of a 'European Springtime'…and although I think most saw this as phoney, it is undeniable that the Chief was seen as a heartthrob by many women and girls – so perhaps the bold gamble paid off? Partly, at least, for everyone knows it is the female sex that, in our day, sets the mood of 'public opinion'.

But other women admired him merely for his 'good looks' – which is like admiring the sun for its roundness, not for its golden scorching fire. Was I, alone of all women, the only one who saw his inner searing flame? That I would like to believe, as it justifies what I am about to do.

Well, when the Chief first arrived in Prague, he was obsessed with the legend of the Golem. He had read Meyrink's famous novel on the aeroplane, and asked if I had also – so I said yes, and bought a copy that afternoon, perusing the strange story for the first time.

Next day I started a conversation, based on my experience of the book. He had read it for the *second* time that night, it turned out – O golden coincidence!

"Miss Sedláková," he said, with intensity barely concealed beneath his formal politeness. "Were you aware that Karel Čapek's play *Rossum's Universal Robots*, also written here in Prague, has many similarities to the legend of the golem? The golem is a man of mud, just like a robot. But, you see, at the end of the play, something occurs that its creators never envisaged. Life always finds a way, and that is what these Curia types will never understand."

"I have read the robot play," I said (truthfully this time).

"And to think this was once the city of *alchemists*," he snarled. "Is their robot-golem a reaction to that, from those afraid of fire? The Curia think *I* am a Golem, you know…a mud-man to clean up their synagogue of Saturdays. Ah well, they'll soon see that they've bitten off more than they can chew, like the sorcerer's apprentice."

"He who manages to bind the golem and refine him will be reconciled with himself," I said, quoting Meyrink to him, and no one can guess my inner turmoil and fluttering heart – but on the outside I was all polite coolness and efficiency, even managing to keep my poise as we read a little from each work, comparing the inner meaning of both authors.

It was unusual for the Chief to engage in such a seemingly frivolous exercise – he was a highly driven young man – but he seemed to place great significence in the golem legend. At the time I didn't understand why, but now that my head is clear it seems that he didn't want a world turned to mud. He believed in a soul. Did that put him at odds with those around him? Yes, of course…

He engaged in plenty of frivolities *outside* of work,

however – and indeed, was expected to. Several times he asked me to accompany him to those decadent parties where the elite unwound.

"Please help to keep me sane," he said. "You're level headed, and I need that in this nest of smiling vipers."

But who can soothe the sun? Anyone who has *been* to one of those parties, can see in their minds' eye what they are like. Full of insane phoney gurus, selling spiritual remedies for all the problems of the multiverse, brought there for amusement by hardcore Praesidium types, but sometimes a novice is taken in and must be disabused. The Servitor Kult was one such, appearing on the scene around this time, but it was more of a trend than a 'kult' – a set of wealthy feminists who suddenly found it cool to be submissive because they thought that no one had done it before, and because they *could*. So they became 24/7 subs (on finding the right master), and played the role enthusiastically. The Curia's Department of Culture issued an official warning against the Servitor Kult, but only a half-hearted one. There were even one or two Curia women involved in it, at least for a few months, before the next trend came along.

And so the Chief was introduced to a Servitor called Darla Shaw, the widow of an ultra-rich currency speculator who had since reverted to her maiden name. She was a smooth operator seeking a harsh master, to keep up with her friends. She was all over the Chief in an instant, and he seemed to enjoy her attentions, despite the fact she was nearly twenty years his senior.

He asked who she was (it was part of my job to be his social navigator), so I whispered her life story into his ear. By the end of the evening she had formally knelt and 'submitted' to him…there were wedding plans afoot, and he had already dictated to me a curt dismissal note for his former betrothed, a Ms. Tricia Philips. He married Darla later that week in a small private ceremony at a country estate outside Prague. His affections for his new bride were not entirely genuine, however. He dropped hints (to me, at least) that he had married her mainly in order to have access to a private fortune (she having inherited the majority of her late husband's wealth, which was valued in the tens of billions).

"I don't enjoy money for its own sake, Miss Sedláková," he told me. "But it's an important resource for my mission." I nodded politely, afraid to ask what his 'mission' was. Later that night I witnessed him whipping his new wife with a curtain rod, and as she writhed in ecstasy beneath his blows, I wished it was *me* that he was beating...but I don't think that's what he meant by 'mission'.

Next evening I accompanied the two of them to a performance of the Czech Philharmonic Orchestra at the Rudolfinum. It was Beethoven's *Triple Concerto*, appropriately enough. The pianist, a thirty-something Chinese with hair that flopped around his face, was a known hater of the Praesidium, and his angry klavier-hammering deadened the impact of the piece. The interplay with the other two lead instruments became a grim battle, but at the same time it helped me to think. It was then that I realised Darla was no *real* threat to me – not a spriritual threat, as only *I* perceived clearly the true inner greatness of the young Octavian. But I longed to hold him in my arms all the same, and this desire has never let up, not for an instant.

After the performance, a man with thick eyeglasses whispered to the Chief of a confidential meeting, one where he would learn something to his advantage. Two days later I was present at this meeting.

"I trust Miss Sedláková implicitly, her discretion is absolute," the Chief said, causing me to glow with pleasure...and even now that I am leaving this world, I maintain this discretion, and will burn this note when my thoughts are collected. *(The note was found unburnt…either she forgot, or the pills kicked in quicker than she intended. – E.J.C.)*

"We know the entire Arts allocation left over from the old EU has just vanished – forty million esperos to be precise – but we don't know where to," said the bespectacled little fellow, and the Chief promised he would look into it promptly.

"I only have the name of a Belgian hedge fund, but there's no hard *proof* linking them with the disappearance of the money," the fellow said. "Just someone who may have known a someone, and so forth. Here's the address and suite number." He scratched something onto a slip of paper.

So next week, the Chief and I flew to Brussels. On the surface it was an educational tour to see how the city had fared after the EU bureaucracy had been dismantled and revamped in Prague. Since its decommision as de facto capital of the EU, Brussels had been trying to reinvent itself as a 'vibrant, cosmopolitan city', just as Bonn had done after German reunification. The only problem was that, with every city now billing itself as vibrant and cosmopolitan, tourists stayed well away. Vibrancy is also also an anonym for 'high crime', and Brussels did not disappoint in that regard.

The glass-honeycomb tombstones of the old European Quarter with its bilingual signage soon gave way to neighbourhoods where an overlap was in place – tongues of the demographic wave, soaking the shores of reason. A decaying, Islamified city, and despite all the noise, an empty feeling underneath, as empty as the cube of Kaaba. The further you walk, the wave actually seems to ride out, like the tide going out before a tsunami. Once the Chief was spat at, and his bodyguards were forced to protect him from what could have been an unpleasant incident.

"And this was once the hometown of that noble

31

reporter Tintin," muttered the Chief. "He would be no more at home here now than would an alchemist in latter day Prague."

After we had walked another few blocks, we reached our intended building – a bland new edifice with a convoluted façade.

"Now," said the Chief, "it's quite possible that certain heads in the Praesidium or Curia know that we're here, investigating this lead, and I want to send a message to them that I'm not a man to trifle with." He instructed his bodyguards to be very rough indeed with the hedge fund's investment manager. "It's something the Curia probably hasn't anticipated. I want it to be crystal clear who has jurisdiction in Europe. Also, I won't tolerate corruption in my fief."

His bodyguards nodded eagerly, but I was surprised. As Executive Commissioner he certainly had powers, but *controlling* the entire European treaty zone? I shivered, suddenly afraid for him.

We quickly found the correct wing of the building. The hedge fund, Gaumont Capital, was listed at the entrance, but the front door was locked. The Chief rang at the buzzer and announced that he was an envoy from the European Department of Culture, who had urgent news to impart to a Mr. Michael Crossley. A minute later a short man in a suit, with slicked back hair and an old-fashioned nose ring, came to the door and ushered us in.

"I'm Crossley," he said in a working-class English accent when we had reached a private office. "Anything the matter?"

There soon was, and he crawled around the floor gasping for breath as the Chief's men smacked him around. "What the *fuck?*" he kept repeating, at weird intervals. "What the fuck have I *done?*"

"Just tell us what happened to the money from the EU Arts Grant."

"Wait…let me guess…someone in Prague told you this…a man called Bernard something."

"Never mind *how* I know."

"Wears glasses, a squinty-eyed bloke. White, but looks like a Chinese moonfish. Big sticky-out ears." An exaggerated but recognisable depiction. "You fool," Crossley snarled. "He's misdirecting you. *He's* the one you should ask about the culture budget. I fucked him over in the past, and this is his revenge on me. He probably feared that with your energy you'd soon be onto him, so he put you on a false trail. All the while he vanishes off to Russia or someplace."

"You're lying."

"No!" There was desperation in his voice, and he really sounded like he meant it.

"Then what will I find in suite 5C of this wing?"

"N-nothing. That's our old office. We moved to *this* suite a few months ago."

"Give me the key to the old office, then. I know you still have it…" It was a bluff, and didn't work, so the Chief had to have recourse to brutality. After they had beaten him within an inch of his life, he finally retrieved an electronic key from the top drawer of his desk, where there were several.

"You can't get away with this. I don't care if you're the Executive Commissioner of the whole fucking world. I have rights…"

"If you tell anyone, you will suddenly cease to exist. And no matter where you hide, we'll track you down."

We marched to the suite, which was empty, but a padlocked trapdoor in the corner drew our attention. The toughs smashed the lock, and we walked down some stairs to find a long, carpeted passage under the ground, like something out of a spy novel.

One bodyguard had a torch, and we followed the passage for what felt like miles. The carpet ended, then our footsteps echoed on clacketty concrete floors. There were no side tunnels. We reached a winding metal staircase going up, and climbed the rusty edifice before reaching a small, dingy chamber with a wooden boarded ceiling, apparently a dead end.

We tapped the walls for secret passages, then realised that there was actually some kind of trapdoor in the ceiling. The bodyguard-built-like-a-mountain pressed his hand against it, and before long there was a splintering sound and it gave. He boosted one of the others up to see if the coast was clear.

"A room without doors," he said. "Just a filing cabinet in the middle." The mountain hauled us up, one after the other, and stayed on guard below. The Chief opened the venetians and peeped out the window of this strange doorless room.

"It looks like we're back in the old EU Quarter," he exclaimed, and was right. The room seemed suddenly filled with ghosts, the dreary shades of the politically correct era. *(She probably refers to the years 2001-2012. – E.J.C.)*

The filing cabinet wasn't locked, and contained a single file. We stood, sat, and squatted patiently while the Chief perused the contents. His eyes grew wider the more he read.

"It isn't tens of millions, it's *hundreds of billions* of esperos that were siphoned away," he whispered in a shocked voice. "And not just the Arts fund, but *most* of the revenue from the old EU."

One of the bodyguards frowned. "Siphoned away where, Chief?"

"I don't know. But Bernard Sauveterre must have been trying to warn me. I should have realised that nothing I learnt during the *Triple Concerto* could be false…only understated," he murmured. "Because three is the magic number."

And then, as we returned to the chambers of the hedge fund, we found that the staff had vanished, documents shredded, computers taken and furniture overturned. And someone had called the Brussels police, who were nonplussed.

"What 'as 'appened 'ere?"

"A crime that can never be atoned for," muttered the Chief.

The mirror-glass on the building opposite now showed a dead city, drained of its last protective energy.

*     *     *

Back in Prague, the Chief walked around with a look of fire. He contacted his Curia liason, and told him about the Arts money (*not* the larger amount – here he winked at me with a fire-swirling eye), and next day attended a meeting with some people from the Unicursal Curia. They asked what he was going to do, and the Chief said "Well, what do *you* suggest?"

"Perhaps a press conference is in order. You must let the public know of this urgent matter at once."

"Good idea," said the Chief, but they couldn't decipher his secret smile.

At the press conference the Chief spoke as follows:

"If I was to announce to you today the disappearance of a large sum of money from the coffers of the old EU…you would be incensed…but I can now reveal…that it is in fact, a…much…*larger*…amount…of…" He spoke at a funereal, drumrolling pace…this was deliberate and calculated, I knew. He told me later, but I already understood. Before further words could emerge from his mouth there was a flurrying of feet, as advisors pretended

35

to whisper in his ear. Someone came to the mic and told the journalists the Executive Commissioner had "urgent unforeseen business, and the press conference must be postponed until tomorrow," then he was whirled out in a flash, leaving his loyal PA behind. I knew what had happened, of course – but was he doing it to test the Curia's resolve of letting him serve his term, or for reasons of justice? (It really *was* a large sum of money.)

I didn't see him until work the next day, when he took me aside and told me in greater detail what had happened.

"I was slapped back, as expected, Miss Sedláková," he said. "It's what the espionage crowd call 'limited hangout'. I was *meant* to find out about that Arts money, and to let the public know. But they didn't foresee that Bernard Sauveterre would tell me more than instructed. He has recently disappeared, needless to say." I shivered – but at the thought of the grey-suited corpses grilling the Chief, like dirty clouds encrusting the sun. (I felt bad for M. Sauveterre of course, but that was purely abstract.)

Next day the conference resumed, and the story of the Arts money was given out to the press, with promises that it would be "looked into severely," with no stone left unturned. That was enough to get them gossiping, accusing and pontificating, ensuring of course that they would never actually muckrake into the real truth of the matter. Limited hangout, indeed.

That evening I walked alone through the Old Town of Prague, fantasizing about what the Chief was doing to his wife. I couldn't live without my sun, and here I was in the moist, clammy labyrinth, with no way out, and night closing in. I ran home sobbing through the cobblestoned streets, and cried myself to sleep. Oh, why couldn't I be a man and die a hero's death? To burn my face in the flames...

But next day I was basking in warmth again – the

Chief instructed me to accompany him on a weekend trip to Munich, where a high-ranking member of the Curia had summoned him to a secret meeting. As we boarded the plane for the short flight, I felt blessed to be alive.

From Munich airport we took a taxi to an Italian restaurant in the university district of Schwabing. The man from the Curia, with a very Jewish-looking face, was waiting at the table he'd reserved for us in a quiet corner.

"Do you like the choice of establishment?" he asked.

"Seems nice enough."

"You don't recognise it? This was *Hitler's* favourite restaurant, you know, in the days when he resided in Munich."

"Really. And why did you want to meet here in particular?"

"Well, Munich in general tends to make me reflect a lot on the past…and this place in particular has that effect." He sighed. "You know, if only Hitler had looked favourably upon the mixing of races, we really could have made use of him."

"It's only his opposition to miscegenation you have a problem with?"

"That's it! That was his problem entirely…not the whole cattle car thing. Now, let's see, I'll have the *coda alla vaccinara*, please." We placed our orders, and chatted over trivial things until the meal arrived. After the repast and a bottle of good Puglian wine, the Curia rep got down to business.

"What I am about to tell you is strictly in confidence. It does not have the official sanction of the Curia, but there are those of us who think you should be on board with it, and we are in the majority." He then told the Chief that, although the Curia distrusted him as a result of the affair of the EU coffers ("and, because we distrust *everyone*," he added with a smile), they nevertheless valued highly his magnetic force and proven leadership ability.

"Combined with your youthful energy, it makes you a veritable *Übermensch*, if you'll excuse the expression. And we would be very foolish indeed not to utilise your talents and persona. We need all the help we can get right now!" I noticed that he didn't say what would happen to the Chief after his 'help' was no longer required.

"How do you want to utilise me, then?"

"Well now, I take it you know our esteemed North American Executive Commissioner…your counterpart on that continent, the delightful Anita Jokum?" A sarcasm, surely, as Ms. Jokum was not only physically repulsive, but had an aggressively self-righteous persona – a real do-gooding harpy.

"I know who she is."

"Well, without mincing words, we wish to be rid of her. Her belligerence has become an embarassment, especially in the USA, which despite its economic decline is still an important country for us. And Anita Jokum has nearly everyone there against her.

"It goes without saying that rightists hate her – pushing a 2010-style political correctness in the 2020s! – but she has also alienated large swathes of the left with her outspoken support for female genital mutilation, despite her claims to be a radical feminist. Not that the American left are especially valuable to us at the moment, mind you…no, the most pressing task at hand is a final crusade to stamp out Islamic fundamentalism, and for that we need to temporarily dispel the resentment of the American Right. We want a showdown, a real clash of civilizations. A last day in the sun for the hamburger-eaters of Flyover Country, before they disappear forever into the melting pot of that good night." His cynicism chilled even me.

"But the Curia or its predecessors *created* fundamentalist Islam," I interjected, unable to help myself, although the Chief had not given me permission to speak.

"Yes, of course, Miss...uh," he said frostily, "but it has outlived its purpose. Like many ideologies we created for strategic reasons, its time is now up. And besides, it has gotten somewhat out of control of late, in case you haven't noticed."

"And Jokum is impeding its demise?" asked the Chief.

"Massively. She just won't be budged on her attempts to appease the fundies, for reasons of her own trendy vanity...a position that scarcely has any traction anymore, not even with the far left. Seriously, can't you feel it in the air, Scarlotti? There has never been a riper time for extreme Islam to perish. *Kairos!*"

"So what do you want me to do?"

"We want you to be our new North American Executive Commissioner, of course. Your talents would be far more valuable over there at the present time."

"You could order me to."

"But it's very difficult for us to stand down an EC without a valid reason, even a continental one like Jokum, let alone the EC of the Praesidium...which technically isn't even in our jurisdiction."

"Technically...but you *could*, though."

"We would prefer it if you didn't give us any reason to."

"Well, there's the Brussels thing. No doubt the reason you want me out of Europe in the first place."

"Come, let's not talk about that. Will you be our man in North America?"

"I'll consider it."

"As EC, you'll need to portray yourself as more right-wing than the current US president. Above all we want you to gain the allegiance of the military, which we will need for our Grand Crusade. And of course your secondary mission will be to bolster the Curia's power over the US as a nation state. Also over Canada and

Mexico."

"Sounds simple. Is that all?"

"Ha, I knew you were the right man for the job! Another bottle of wine, please, waiter. The Chianti this time, I think..."

\*     \*     \*

After that, it all seemed to happen so fast.

Anita Jokum was forced to stand down over a sordid sex scandal. You saw it on the gossip shows, no doubt...the video shot in an expensive brothel showing its employee (a mulatto girl) threatened with clitoridectomy by Jokum if the former didn't bring her to climax in time for her committee meeting that afternoon; not to mention footage of Jokum whipping the unfortunate whore with a riding crop, hollering that she would "tan her nigger hide back to the sugar cane fields" if she didn't admit that "niggers are superior to white liberals like me. *You are the master race*...just admit it, you lying slut..."

"Please, stop hitting me so hard."

Of course there was no proof that the brothel itself released the footage...normally such an incident involving a high-ranking Curia official would have been covered up immediately, but *someone* apparently wanted it released. That, along with other tidily leaked 'incidents', brought about the downfall of Anita Jokum. Maximillian Scarlotti was appointed Interim Commissioner, pending immediately.

The Chief then let it be known he was sponsoring a law and order campaign aimed at stamping out the Knockout Game, a sport that had been growing in popularity for two decades, and which had now reached unprecedented levels of brutality. The sport, also known as the Polar Bear Hunt, invariably involved a group of young black men approaching a solitary white victim, and seeing how quickly they could knock him (or increasingly *her*) to the ground. Death on impact was considered a high score, but there were other ways to amass points, such as creatively kicking the victim to death, or varied mutilations.

The media had been instrumental in covering up the existence of this sport, but the more victims there were, the more people knew of it…so finally, despite the best efforts of Anita Jokum to play things down, Euro-Americans had begun to reach boiling point.

Into this tense pre-storm atmosphere flew the Chief. He travelled to Philadelphia, myself at his side, to be photographed with Knockout victims who had survived the experience, and thereby immediately endeared himself to a large segment of the population.

As expected, this provoked massive violent protests from the far left worldwide, especially in Europe where he was still offically EC.

Something we *didn't* expect, however, was that the Reformed Ku Klux Klan (now open to members of all races and sexual inclinations) would also protest against the Chief for "inciting disharmony among the community of the nations." A group of Reformed Klansmen actually burnt a huge wooden rainbow outside the hotel in Fishtown where we were staying…it was an eerie sight, those hooded figures screeching about 'social justice', while the black police moved them on.

After that we were driven to Rockville, Maryland (a suburb of Washington, D.C.), where we attended a meeting in a nondescript office building with a blustering gentile neocon who thought he was more important than he actually was. I can't remember the details, but apparently the meeting was successful.

Then we crossed the Potomac into Arlington and met with some senior military figures, and that seemed to go well too. I think the Chief wanted their support over and above that of the current US president – the line between nationalism and globalism becoming ever more blurred. You remember that President Hodge's election over the Democratic incumbent in 2020 caused the worst Black and Hispanic riots in US history...but he has since proved a more malleable figure for the Curia, ironically, than Anita Jokum herself.

Nevertheless, the Curia needs a *real* captain at the wheel for the coming Crusade, and that's where the Chief steps in...

So, shortly afterwards he was formally appointed North American Executive Commisioner. He never set foot in Prague again after his first day in the USA, and when I went to his office to report for work one morning he was gone...whisked off somewhere and given a new PA. So now I am back in Prague, which is a living tomb without him.

Time for my last lines: I am going to God now, and if I return to earth, let it be an earth where my golden template has triumphed.

Let me stare untrembling into the face of the unconquered Sun.

*(Karina Sedláková was found dead of a sleeping pill overdose in her apartment near Wenceslas Square, Prague. – E.J.C.)*

3

## THE TESTIMONY OF
## MAJOR GENERAL JOHN C. FRAMPTON

Dear Marcus,

It's been too long, hasn't it? I guess you know how busy I've been, but now that I finally have some time I'll try to fill you in on what has been happening. I can't posit every detail, for security reasons of course, but will simply endeavor to run you down on the main cut and thrust.

You've heard all about the Crisis, and you've also heard, no doubt, how I was assigned as Scarlotti's liaison to the Pentagon by the former Secretary of Defense (on the recommendation of the Joint Chiefs of Staff). I was surprised that their recommendation was accepted, especially given my previously expressed (albeit cautious) optimism as to the man himself. I expected they would want someone more cynical, but apparently I was wrong.

Things have sure been getting strange in the Beltway of late. Those conservatives who were most vocal these past few years in their opposition to the Curia have now suddenly decided they want Scarlotti as their head of state over that "miserable son of a bitch" Hodge (as one of them described him to me in private).

"Pity he (Scarlotti)'s not eligible for president, as foreign-born," growled another. And I'm not talking Paleos, Libertarians or White Nationalists (whose ranks are swelling fast enough), but your common or garden Republican. It shows how deep the distrust of Neocons is right now – especially ironic given that Hodge's biggest election promise was to *counter* the power of the Curia, something he has singularly failed at. I almost suspect the Curia are using the two as rivals, to find out which is best: the unpredictable genius (Scarlotti) or the dumb puppet (Hodge).

Scarlotti's swearing-in was a real eye-opener. I don't mean the austere public ceremony – there was also a lavish *private* do, up here in Manhattan, and I tell you I couldn't have dreamt this thing up. Scarlotti actually *prostrated* himself before the current head of Curia, donning a yarmulke before 'singing' a two minute piece of gangsta rap (which presumably they made him memorize in advance) about pimping someone's sister out for KFC and crack. He was toasting shalom and shaking his rump like a goddamn baboon, can you imagine? I don't know how that would gel with his public opposition to the knockout game – is it actually some weird initation rite, or do these Curia bastards just have a *really* sick sense of humor?

Anyhow, over the subsequent week I got to know Scarlotti about as well as anyone *can* know him, but he still remains an enigma to me. About the only sign of humanity I saw in him was when he learnt that his former secretary in Europe had taken her own life – he seemed depressed, then; but the next day was sanguine as usual.

Then came the Crisis.

It's hard to tell it objectively from my own standpoint, as I was in the thick of it, carrying messages and intrigues back and forth like the god Mercurius. My time was spent in a dizzying oscillation between the skyscrapered canyons of Manhattan and the domed velveteen skies of Arlington. I found myself longing for change, and when a middle of the road guy like me starts to feel that a revolution might be good, you know the country is in serious trouble – that is, if it even *is* a 'country' any more. Scarlotti will either save or damn us. Or maybe both.

I don't believe the Chiefs of Staff share my musings in any sense, but the sheer *hatred* they've developed towards Israel is striking. Their talk is now of not wasting another single bullet on the 'parasite state' (as many now call it). And these were men handpicked by the Curia!

I won't say any of them have gone as far as to express sympathy for the Palestinian cause, as that would be out of keeping with their character (and mine), but distrust of Israel, yes…that's now the glue keeping our military united, from the lowest grunt up to (and there's no point hiding this now he's gone public) the former Secretary of Defense himself.

"$10 million a day to that shithole," was the comment he was forced to resign over, caught by an open mic, but I could tell you other, more extreme things that he said in private. And again, this was a man who had been picked by the Curia, *founded* by all accounts because the old UN was too anti-Zionist.

So what did the Joint Chiefs of Staff want from Scarlotti? Simply his assurance that America won't be bogged down in another Zionist war without honor. And to our surprise, Scarlotti readily agreed to this.

"I have big plans for this world, gentlemen," he said, "but Zionist wars aren't among them." So he gave us his word of honor, which still counts for something among the military, if not among politicians.

This greenlighted us to give the flick to Hodge, that dumb shill of a sock puppet who has been worse than disappointing. He spluttered and raged, both privately and publicly, but was helpless to prevent something that could never previously have been imagined, let alone thought possible – *the direct allegiance of the US military to the Curia*, freezing the President out. In our age of blurred jurisdictions and ambiguous globalization no one should have been surprised at how easily it was pulled off.

The central committee of the Curia themselves, of course, claimed to be opposed to Scarlotti's actions – but were they? Perhaps by the *motives* of the Chiefs of Staff, who had such a disturbing change of heart (was it the 'OpenBorders4Israel' campaign, or the neverending sea of atrocities?), but Scarlotti himself assured us they would leave us alone, as long as they thought he was using the military for their bizarre project of "stamping out extreme Islam" (more on that later).

Scarlotti is energetic, even his worst enemies concede that, and he immediately commenced to "make the forces strong again," succeeding alarmingly in the task. His first act was to expel cannabis users and the overweight, which immediately reduced the enlisted ranks by half. Then he weeded out all those belonging to the Crips and Bloods, for presumed disloyalty, reducing the remainder by nearly half again.

Then, he did something more controversial. He announced his intention to ban women from serving in the armed forces proper, instead proposing the creation of an auxillery services branch, as in the WWII days. While I don't know of any *man* in the forces who would be opposed to this in their heart of hearts, many let their token protests resound in the media for fear of not doing so. And then came the protests from the far left. Yes, the anti-imperialist, anti-military-industrial left are currently having conniptions because the fairer sex *may* be removed from frontline combat ops, proving officially that the world is now *beyond* being 'beyond satire' and has in fact become a neverending satire in itself. But of what, I don't rightly know.

Anyway, with the ranks of our regular forces down to 28% (19% if his female policy goes through), Scarlotti had to explain to the Curia how he would be able to persuade America to go a-crusading. But although the ranks have been thinned, morale is now at an all time high! I almost think Scarlotti could persuade the general staff to commit to *anything*, even if he reneged on his promise not to lead us into any more Zionist wars!

At the time, he confided to the Joint Chiefs of Staff (via myself) something which is no longer a secret, that he has been recruiting a legion of bloodthirsty pirates from the Horn of Africa to serve him in the capacity of a private army, undisciplined but incredibly fierce, thanks to his wife's considerable fortune.

And in the midst of all this, he somehow found time to embark on a pet project of his, the establishment of a university whose aim is to develop something called the 'Glass Bead Game'.

"Yes, I know the game is only supposed to be a metaphor for creativity, Frampton," he told me. "But I'm interested in whether *the attempt itself* might not revivify Western culture." And then he launched into a long and confusing ramble about hieroglyphs that stood for multiple things; for instance, certain musical chords and the chemical structure of Portland cement. I didn't pretend to know what he was jabbering on about, and still don't.

But then came the second Crisis. I was standing by Scarlotti's side when his wife fell to the assassin's bullet. I have seen men die, but never a woman, and it's not something I will ever forget. I remember her trying to form some last hissing words, which never emerged. She looked at Scarlotti as if begging him to rescue her, before her eyes went away to the dark beyond. Scarlotti was weeping, yet rigid and composed. Was the bullet meant for him? Who fired it? Still unanswered questions...

After this, he became understandably more cautious, expending much effort in creating what he regarded as an invincible bodyguard. By now the leftists and their media enablers were inciting serious mass riots against

47

him, mainly because of his attempts to stamp out the Knockout Game. He adroitly used the Baltimore riots as an excuse to bring down martial law across the continent, something neither we of the forces or, I believe, the average Joe, were particularly enamored of. But we didn't know what he would do with his temporary discretionary powers! You've seen for yourself the laws he has made – making left-wing race-agitators live amongst those they claim to be helping, for instance. We've all been waiting a long time for that one…

Naturally, the Curia were incensed. They must have felt like Frankenstein, with the monster they created now getting well out of hand. All the more so when he disappeared for a week and came back with a blushing new bride – no other than Kahina Tate, daughter of Mohammed Tate, emir of the Provisional Emirate of Northern Iraq and Syria (PENIS).

Despite his Arab first name, this post-ISIS emir is as white as a swan, a blue-eyed blond originally from the High Atlas (said to be of Berber stock, with an English father that he never knew, and, I suspect, a healthy admixture of Visigothic blood). This icy warlord has done much to heal and reorganize the war-ravaged lands of northern Iraq, and is much hated by the Curia as a result. In some ways he seems a kindred spirit of Scarlotti, so perhaps it should be unsurprising that they formed an alliance, though for the life of me I couldn't tell you how it came about; Scarlotti likes to play things close to the chest.

The wedding was a signal to the Curia – they immediately began to hook their claws into India and the Russian 'dissident' factions. Perhaps they are biding their time, waiting for Scarlotti's predicted mideast war absence (which he *did* promise) in order to check his power here in the US.

And this week, Scarlotti has announced (allegedly

against the wishes of his father-in-law) the creation of a new homeland for the Palestinians, a plan to help them to self-sufficiency in a fertile region made empty by the Iraq wars. Israel is *livid* at this, proving beyond all doubt (to myself at least) that they enjoy brutalizing Arabs (besides needing them for menial labour), and Scarlotti told them so in as many words.

"You'll just have to learn to live *without* servants," he bellowed at the Israeli envoy. Due to this, I like him immensely, but there is still a feeling of ambiguity at the bottom of my heart. I'll say it again: Scarlotti will save or damn us, or both.

At least we now live in interesting times once more...

## 4

## THE TESTIMONY OF
## OLENA PETRENKO
(via extracts from her journal)

Childhood is bound like the Gordian knot with my memories of the Black Sea, and I still feel its waters welling up within me today. Sometimes these waters are leaden, as grey as the military ships that sail on their curved expanses, and sometimes they are blue as pigmented cobalt. Then would come dusk, when I would sit and watch the seabirds waver to shore, flitting from open waters to the quiet empty vastlands in darkening spaces behind me, the same birds Ovid once saw during his exile, perhaps; and the same waters the Argonauts crossed searching for the fleece of renewal.

And out in the distance, invisible, the towering heights of Caucasus, where once-bright memories of the fire-thief have transmuted into something weird and many-faceted, and beyond these, pitch-black Karabakh in dolorous Armenia.

But king in my mind are legends of my own land – those of the mighty Bogatyr, so nameless and dread, whose Arrow brought war and suffering. He commanded his sons to throw this Arrow into the depths of the Black Sea, for they lacked the strength to wield it themselves, and that is why its waters are always restless.

And just lately, it seems, the Bogatyr has returned.

These last few years, until yesterday, everything has been so empty in Kiev, falling into a void. The old places that once meant much to me seemed drained of blood and meaning, like a plastic bubble-pack sucked out with a ridiculous vacuum. Even the mysterious fire of metal bands I used to admire was gone, and in interviews they now seemed empty imperialists.

But Kiev wasn't always like this – it once felt full of mystery and promise.

*Was that just an illusion?* Either this mystery never existed (then whence comes my memory of it?), or it *did* exist then disappeared (then why and where did it go?); and either way there is something unknown, unseen at work. A god or a demon mocks me. The only other alternative is that 'I' myself don't exist, but I can't accept that. So I would sigh, and say "the season of autumn is upon us," and other precious things like that, and my mother would look at me like I was mad.

"Why don't you follow your sister?" she would badger me. "She makes good money in America." But I shot her a look of withering scorn every time she broached this hated topic, although it failed to silence her. Nothing did…except when I would bark back, nagging her about Natalya's upbringing, and then she would take on a look of pouting indifference, pressing grey lips together til they were greyer still, an ashy tight communism. It seemed the world now *belonged* to people like her.

Then Anna, who I hadn't seen in ages, phoned and asked me to come to a hall in central Kiev and hear a speech. It was the North American Potentate for the Curia (or something like that), she said…and I told her coldly that I had no interest in such things.

She laughed and said: "This one is different," then

hung up. I didn't know if she referred to the speech or the man, but her tone had struck me dumb with curiosity. So I went, endeavouring to see what was on the cards.

I had no idea that the fire would return to my heart last night!

The Bogatyr (for so I now think of him) was visiting Kiev with his Praetorians, the elite bodyguard he had created after his wife was assassinated, by a bullet said to be meant for him, and he was here to negotiate. He doesn't wish for open war, yet refuses to guarantee or confirm the new Ukrainian constitution until his authority in this land is recognised.

However: I didn't care about any of this. I only cared for his electrifying speech.

In his speech he *talked* of the Bogatyr, speaking openly of a Slavic legend that until then had gone unspoken in my heart, but instead of destroying this myth, *his* light seemed to make it grow! I feel sure he is sent as an Avatar from our gods…perhaps the Avatar of the entire Slavic folk, though he isn't Slav himself.

"*My* imperialism embraces ethnic and regional differences and boundaries," he thundered. "Unlike the phoney imperialism of Sheldon Albright, that traitor to humanity, with his open borders madness…" That drew a rousing cheer from the crowd, as Albright is powerful and supremely hated. And then the Bogatyr denounced some of our own Ukrainian nationalists as dupes, playing into the hands of Curia and Albright.

"But you're part of the Curia yourself!" someone shouted.

"I AM the Curia," grinned the Bogatyr. "And don't let anyone tell you otherwise. But now I am steering it in a *different direction*."

How firmly and adamantly he stated this! And I knew that here was a man to be trusted, an agent of the virile gods themselves. And Anna thought so, too, as she

---

danced towards me through the crowd, her face aglow with the flames of future.

"And well," she shouted, "wasn't I right to summon you?" I laughed merrily, taking her hand and leading her through the throng to somewhere we could talk more peaceably, but when we reached the park around the corner, the words just wouldn't came…only tears at our own rebirth.

And when I got home, I thought how flabby my drunken father looked compared to the Bogatyr. I had a sudden feeling he was already dead, and that if I planted a tree atop his grave, it too would grow to a living death, and so on for seven generations until, finally, a green sapling would emerge from the shadow of its petrified forbears…seven generations to break down the corpse.

But for me, the lightning is shaping a different world entirely.

[…]

Now many Ukrainians are volunteering for the Bogatyr's 'International Brigade' (even this name infuriates the Unicursal Curia, who seem to believe they have a monopoly on the international) and also the more elite Praetorian Guard. I myself have volunteered for the women's auxilleries, and will learn in two days if I am accepted or not. Even if rejected (unlikely, as I am sound in body and soul), I will find some other way to help the Bogatyr to glory. But I very much wish to be accepted for the auxilleries, as part of their task is spreading propaganda, which appeals to me immensely. Although the Bogatyr encourages traditional roles of wife and motherhood, I feel I can contribute in other ways at this point, and it seems that so do many other young women…the Bogatyr is loved!

[…]

Yesterday was the proudest day of my life – accepted into the brigades of Bogatyr! – but my mother had to sour the taste with a shallow argument, repeated from the propaganda of the Curia news machine:

"He will betray us. He is negotiating with Russia, to lock us into a definite sphere of Russian economic influence…"

"And, what if he is? He has extracted a guarantee from the Russians to leave Ukrainian *culture*, including neopagans like me, alone. And do you honestly think economics is more important than culture?"

"You can combine them. Your sister is in the movies, for instance…"

"In *porno* movies, in Los Angeles."

"At least it's money."

"It will destroy her soul, if she still has one."

"You are a vicious girl. I am ashamed of you."

"Well, at least I'm not corrupt." And then she snorted like a pig, leaving the room.

Truly, she does not understand.

She understands *nothing*.

[…]

The Bogatyr is succeeding in driving a wedge between the Ukraine administration and the 'official' Curia, but he has been less successful in the west and south Slavic lands. So now the Curia begins to play the role of mediator between the 'Bloc' (Croatia, Poland etc.) and the Bogatyr. It is difficult, because there has been a resurgence of the Western style 'left' in these countries: marches against the Archetype begun in Germany have spread outwards…but not to Ukraine, thank the gods!

Meantime, my parents try every trick in the book to make me quit the Brigade. They even cut me out a newspaper article about a big pagan festival in Lithuania, hoping to entice me there and away from Bogatyr…but my fealty to him *is* paganism in its purest state, somewhere flaccid festivals cannot pierce. For he is the Bogatyr.

And I am distressed, too, because I sense my parents' emptiness…how awful it must be for them! I wonder what they will take with them when they depart this plane of being? Just wasted time, dank and crumbling…

There was a moment only yesterday when I wondered if they might be right, and maybe *I* am going mad…and then I returned to the Brigade, and realised without doubt *we* are the sane ones!

In the end, they will see so too.

[…]

Arguments coming thick and fast now. Myself and mother, Bogatyr and Curia, each reflecting the other.

My father's depression and alcoholism are now established beyond doubt, and he is increasingly comfortable with them – until someone cuts off his supply of vodka, of course. I wanted to, but couldn't. Too soft and afraid of hurting him, but more damage to him in the long run. So should I steel myself to the task, worthy of Bogatyr?

Then, these constant fights with my mother on her

raising of Natalya, my sister's little girl. Mother is determined to surround the infant with the worst of Western trash, and with newfound strength I berate her:

"What is the purpose of these dolls?"

"To play with, of course."

"Do they *look* Ukrainian, with their plastic eyes and muddy features blended from every race on earth?"

"Please don't tell me you're a racist as well as unpatriotic!"

"What? Racist *and* unpatriotic? How is that possible?"

"We know you are unpatriotic because you follow that awful Scarlotti…and you're racist because you also appear to have a problem with certain dolls…"

"They are disgusting. They're not a *real* race, they're artificial."

"It's such a shame you feel that way. They are what every normal girl plays with."

"And who's pushing them? The Curia!"

"I don't understand your politics."

"I just want every people to be proud and free…and Imperium guarantees that."

"I'm sorry, my girl, but you are racist and unpatriotic, and I scarcely recognise you any longer. I really don't know what has happened to my second favourite daughter."

Insults aside, she had everything the wrong way round, just like we were in mirror-backward universes! But as she said her piece, something boomed from the TV news which caused me to quiver in trepidation. The game has now begun in earnest:

"A spokesman for the Unicursal Curia today announced the organisation's official severance of North American Executive Comissioner Maximillian Scarlotti, who, however, is refusing to stand down, claiming that he represents a made-up fantasy body called the *Multicursal* Curia. This deluded man's ravings have caused great sadness to the world body, and to the humankind it represents."

So now the Curia and their controlled networks (in other words *all* the networks) were busy denouncing the Bogatyr as a 'traitor'. Israel was displeased with him, despite his avowal of 'the rights of peoples' (what does that matter to them?), and the news footage showed many Orthodox Jews wailing and gnashing their teeth…as if anyone cared! So now "war is declared, you'd better come down," and the world stands blinking on the razor's edge. Will the Bogatyr's sons find strength to wield his arrow?

[…]

I wanted to take mother to the Black Sea, so she could sense the Bogatyr's rebirth for herself, but her eyes clouded over when I told her of the legend. "Oh, that old story," she said woodenly, and I knew then, finally, that she is lost. I wept for her soul, and at the end felt closure. There is nothing I can do for her, her soul will drift to mist, so just find comfort in that. The real world now is Brigade, and my happy friendships therein.

And now I know I possess the strength to launch legal proceedings, to take my sister's child away from its grandparents' care.

It will be a Brigade baby, and facilities will be provided for it. Legends, too, more nourishing than milk…for the Bogatyr is rising.

## 5

## THE TESTIMONY OF
## HARLAN COAD
(via his journal)

Cobain Day in Aberdeen today…hooray.

The first Cobain Day I really remember was the big one of 2017, the time it was made an offical public holiday. But Hoquiam celebrates it in April, a different day to us, and someone on the Aberdeen council said that made it too close to Hitler's birthday. That's when the trouble started, and the deputy mayor of Hoquiam was stabbed in the arm so the dark blood gushed.

After recovering, he apologized for his microagressions, and Cobain Day had been a pretty quiet affair ever since. Hoquiam council now spell it Kobain Day (as 'Kurdt' sometimes spelled his own name that way), but there has been no more violence.

I always feel cynical around this time. Except for the ritual hymn 'Something in the Way' at the bridge-sleeping ceremony, they never even play the guy's music, and the whole thing seems like a big wank-fest. But I would hate for people to think I'm down on the guy. Besides the fact that Naomi likes him, he also had a good effect on at least one 'alienated loner' I used to know – Dobbin. The Nirvana song 'Tourettes' encouraged Dobbin to take up painting, and maybe he would be dead now if it wasn't for that. But Dobbin is the exception, not the rule, and hardly anyone listens to that kind of music anymore. The only thing that matters to most people is that drugs are *fully legal* in Aberdeen this one day of the year, and that's why I'm sitting here smoking a joint under the bridge as I write.

Soon a dozen others will be here for the bridge-sleeping ceremony, when the mayor lies down symbolically in the freezing mud...but I'll be well gone before then. I might walk over to the most recent statue, the one started four years ago that was never finished (and probably never will be), half-formed, with birdshit under its eyes like crocodile tears. Honestly, it looks more like Gollum from *The Lord of the Rings* than Kurt. They say they stopped building it because the tourists stopped coming – but I don't remember a time when they actually did. Even the 2017 ceremony was just a local affair.

And now, ten years later, the whole town seems empty. Naomi is gone, and we're all devastated, especially me. I really want to marry that girl, and I only realized it after she was gone. She's probably in some library in Olympia right now, working on her thesis. No, wait, she hasn't graduated yet, she intends to write a thesis on Kurt *after* she graduates...now I remember. She's the only one I know who's literally obsessed with our town's tutelary spirit, old murdered Kurt. He'd be sixty if he lived today, and hardly anyone here remembers him as a real person – if he ever actually was one. Some folk even think it's a conspiracy and he never existed at all. Not my grandmother, though – she thinks she may have seen him once, around 1986, cutting his toenails in the main street, just a couple of years before my mother was born, and before he was famous.

Mom, who's still politically correct years after it went out of fashion, once made a remark about how she read 'In Bloom' is an ironic song, and it was even more ironic that jocks would sing along to it when it was really an attack on them. That's what she'd read, anyway.

59

But as she said it, Grandma looked thoughtful, as if remembering an old crush.

So, I used to fantasize that Kurt was actually my grandfather, which would be better than the truth.

But I have to admit I find it hard to grasp the guy. Could he actually have been a real person, and if so then why did they make a fucking statue out of him?

These questions will probably never be answered…

[…]

Dobbin is joining the Dreamers and Poets Brigade. I record a conversation around the dinner table for posterity…the weirdest one ever, in which I saw a whole new side to Grandma.

Grandma: "What is the Dreamers and Poets?"

Me: "It's part of Scar-Lo's International Brigade."

Mom: [Snorting sound.]

Grandma: "And what is the International Brigade?"

Me: "It has generous wages, but tough training and discipline. The Dreamers and Poets is for artists, though, and it's more lenient. Scar-Lo is trying to get them to join in the fight against globalism or something. I think he's hoping to attract the Wolves of Joy. I dunno if they'll bite, though."

Mom: "If you had ever buried your own child, you would hate and despise that kind of horseshit." [She actually said horseshit.] "Scarlotti's a troublemaker."

Me: "You don't still blame me for that?" [It was a reference to my twin sister Kathy, who died in early childhood, less real to me even than Kurt]. "What's that got to do with Scarlotti?"

Mom: "How many children is *he* going to kill? He's making war."

Me: "Isn't war better than tyranny?"

Mom: "*Harlan!* What's gotten into you?"

Me: "The Curia have gotten out of hand. They're pushing everyone around."

Mom: "Maybe that's because they're trying to stamp out racism, sexism, transphobia…"

Me: "They're just words, Mom."

Mom: "You wouldn't say that if you saw a person of color being bullied…"

Me: "I don't think I'd see that, because they're more likely to be doing the bullying."

Mom: "*Harlan!*" [Nearly choking on her GMO salad.]

Grandma: "I'm afraid he may be right. Haven't you heard of this knockout game business?"

Mom: "A vile myth of the corporate media."

Me: "No, the media did their best to cover it up. But what's any of this got to do with Scar-Lo? He supports the right of *all* peoples to exist and thrive, doesn't he?"

Mom: "Yeah, separately, in little Nazi enclaves."

Me: "No, he's said there can also be mixed enclaves for people who want a multicultural homeland."

Mom: "*Everyone* should have a multicultural homeland."

Me: "So it can be as soulless as Seattle?"

Mom: "Aberdeen is more soulless."

Me: "How come it inspired Cobain to write his songs, then?"

Mom: "He hated it here. That's why he moved to Olympia."

Grandma: "I'm afraid that's not strictly true. He moved to Olympia because of pussy."

Mom: "*Mother!*"

Me: [Snickering.]

Grandma: "You shouldn't be so uptight, dear. Anyway, it was *politically correct* pussy by all accounts…the kind Olympia is famous for. So you can relax."

Me: "And what do *you* think about Scar-Lo, Grandma?"

Grandma: "Everything is so dreary just now, Harlan. Maybe you should join the Dreamers and Poets brigade yourself. You've done some writing, haven't you?"

Mom: "*Mother!*"

Grandma: "Put a sock in it."

Mom: "Encouraging him to join a fascist cult!"

Me: "I guess I'll see what Dobbin thinks of it."

Grandma: "Isn't that a bit insipid, waiting for someone *else* to test the water? Where is the fire of youth?"

Me: [Blushing bright red.]

Mom: "I can't believe I'm hearing this. In my own house."

Grandma: "It's a rented house. And if you believe Harlan has any prospects in a world dominated by the Curia, then you're out of your fucking mind, girl."

Mom: [Storms away from the table in disgust.]

Grandma: "Just consider what I said, Harlan. You have to grasp the nettle if you want to be happy. My biggest mistake was not realizing that in time. There's still hope for you, though."

So I went down to the basement and put some King Diamond onto the antique turntable ("*Grandma, welcome home!*") to thank her for her honesty. (A much better singer than Kurt, IMHO).

[…]

Forget Mom's fascist paranoia about Scar-Lo. I met my first *real* Nazi today. Not a German one, though. He was from a group called North West Front, founded by a guy called Covington sometime last century. This Nazi

62

called himself a 'white nationalist', but they're the ones the media call Nazis, right?

Anyway, night was falling over Aberdeen and I decided to take the bus home. The bus was nearly full, and this large stocky man in a camo jacket sat down next to me, that is, in the aisle seat opposite to my aisle seat, and I had a sudden vision of blood. Everything seemed to go red. Then, half a minute later, he got into an argument with the couple in front of him, who were talking about President Hodge.

"I think the president is doing his best in a tricky situation," the man was saying.

"Lies!" bellowed the Nazi. At first I thought he was drunk, but his speech was clear, just highly exhuberent. "You've been listening to the Ziomedia, haven't you? Hodge belongs in a mental asylum, along with his corrupt cuckservative lackeys."

"No offence, buddy, but I was talking to my wife, not to you."

"Well, we're in the end times, pal, so no need to stand on ceremony. I won't apologize for speaking my mind, that's for damn sure." For some reason I was anxious to defuse the situation, perhaps because his bellowing was interrupting my lovelorn musings about Naomi.

"Do you really think we're in the *end times?*" I asked politely.

"Hey, buddy, this could be the last bus ride we ever take."

"Why…is there a bomb in your jacket?" I chuckled nervously.

"Do I *look* like a terrorist?"

"Um…"

"Oh, so you think I look like the *media* type of a terrorist, is that it? Always a white man, isn't it? So utterly realistic…" His vocal chords dive-bombed with sarcasm. "No, if *I* had a bomb we'd all be fucking dead by now. I don't mess around. Lucky for you, though, I'm the honorable type. I only kill with fists, knives or guns, and only then when absolutely necessary."

I believed him. And then he started telling me about his organization, which I admit made me a bit uncomfortable. The other passengers were doing their best to ignore him, glancing timidly only when they rose to get off the bus.

Put bluntly, the guy aims to set up a 'White Republic' here in the Pacific Northwest, but amidst all his political talk I learnt something highly interesting: it seems that his people have offered Scar-Lo the 'Honorary Presidency' of their North West Republic.

"He's not WN strictly speaking, but he stands for the *rights of peoples*, including whites."

I was all like 'whoa', but inside I felt far less cynical, even touched. Sometimes I wish I had the 'alphaness' of these people, any of them! Scar-Lo, the Nor'westers, the Wolves of Joy…hell, even my PC mother has more balls than I do. Grandma was right, perhaps it *is* time to grasp the nettle. But how do I do it?

The bus was getting closer to home, and by now it was nearly empty.

For some reason, I asked what he thought of the Wolves of Joy.

"Unreliable," he snorted. From his talk I gathered that the Nor'westers were more conservative than the Wolves. Also, the Wolves originally started as a rebellion against 'boomers' (Grandma's generation), who are now dying off and irrelevant…or that's what the Nazi thinks, anyhow.

"Look I'll admit that the boomers squandered a lot," he said, "but you have to move on, and besides, later generations aren't any better. A lot of the gripes about boomers have to do with them locking up all the wealth, and those kinds of materialist concerns are beneath the dignity of the North West Front."

"But the Wolves themselves have transcended their anti-boomer origins, haven't they?"

"Maybe," he muttered.

"And they're anti-colonialist, and so are you."

"Maybe," he muttered again.

My stop was coming up. It was the last stop, and I realized in horror that he must be getting off here too! We stepped off the bus, out into the rotting night. He walked along with me for a bit before I got the courage to say: "Uh, do you live round here?"

"Huh?" He looked round, confused. "Truth be told, I don't even remember where I was going…"

"We're right on the edge of town. If you wait on the next street there'll be a bus back to Cobain Plaza before too long."

"Nah, think I'll just walk. I'm an animal, really, I feel cooped up on a bus. Not even sure why I was on it to begin with." And with that he turned and trudged across the vacant wasteland to the next street, right though a big clump of *stinging nettles*.

My time approacheth, surely…

[…]

The trip to Olympia was hardly what you would call a success. I wanted to win her over with words…words of steel, words of adamant, words of barbed wire and monkeys' brains…but I couldn't even find her, and the events of the world kept impinging. I wandered around the campus of the Evergreen State College in a daze, for I don't know how long, as afternoon turned to night, and then a security guard approached shining a torch into my face.

He said: "I won't bother asking you for ID as it's clear you're not a student…now scram, or I'll hold you til the cops get here. And you don't want *them* to get involved."

I'm not sure how he knew that I wasn't an Evergreen student…maybe your physiognomy changes when you take classes there…but I left before this shambling ape tossed its nose further into my field of flowers. I'm the last person to cause a scene.

So I caught a bus downtown and checked into a hostel. The TV in the foyer blared out some unexpected news: a serious outbreak of Ebola had occurred among Scar-Lo's troops. I still don't know what to think of Scar-Lo, but the news depressed me in some phantasmic way.

I got to the twelve-bed dorm, and some guy had put a tablecloth round his bunk (I could see his dreadlocks poking out), and was smoking a substance that smelt like burning cowshit. That depressed me still further, so I went for a walk outside to collect my thoughts.

On the dark street at the other side of the block I rounded a corner only to have more torches shine into my eyes, this time from what turned out to be two black cops. I answered their grim questions submissively, half-paranoid they were telepathic, and knowing they were waiting for the slightest excuse to beat me down. Eventually they got bored, so I hurried back to the hostel, relieved to have escaped unmaimed.

The next day I returned to Evergreen in full sunshine, mingling with the collegiate body in a spirit of friendship…but they seemed very sedate compared with my image of what college students are supposed to be like. Maybe they all had hangovers? I got some odd frowns, particularly from females, increasing my paranoia that my physiognomy really *did* look out of place, and, after one last look around for Naomi (there wasn't any sign of her), I'm sorry to say that I fled that sterile place, heart pounding with fear.

I thought of having another go tomorrow, so paid for one more night at the hostel. This time the TV in the foyer announced that Scar-Lo himself has contracted Ebola! There is chaos, apparently, and no one knows what is going on.

Although I can't compare my miserable problems to Scar-Lo's, this certainly matched how I felt.

Back in the dorm, the stinking hippy had moved on and his bed was taken by two Chinese girls (not lesbians, just top and tailing) who had left their evening dinner (raw fish) on the table with flies crawling all over it. This didn't seem to bother them…but I confess I went to the john and puked everywhere (probably a reaction to my horrible day, not to the flyblown fish). Anyway, next morning I decided to leave the disgusting city of Olympia, which makes Aberdeen feel clean and welcoming by comparison.

What did Kurt see in this dump? Grandma must be right, the guy must have moved here for 'pussy' as she delicately put it. As for Naomi, who am I kidding? I love her, but she's better off without a loser like me. Time to move on. A fire of pride now burns inside me, even stronger than the pangs of unrequited love.

The morning paper in the foyer told me that presidential forces are now seeking to regain control of what Scar-Lo dubbed the 'American Protectorate,' now that he himself is out of action and almost certainly dying.

It seems Scar-Lo has alienated the right-wingers lately by raising taxes to pay for his Brigades, although he also put an *extra special* tax on 'rich leftists', which caused a lot of hysteria. So nearly everyone is against him…all the blabbermouths, anyway…what a guy! On my way back to the Aberdeen bus I heard some snoots outside a posh café making catty remarks about him, and one of them called him an 'ignorant redneck'.

Hold on, this guy is supposed to have been the greatest scholar of his time! I'd hate to know what these snoots would say about *me* behind my back.

[...]


Scar-Lo has recovered!

The doctors are announcing it as a virtual miracle, as it seems no one had ever made a *full* recovery from such advanced Ebola before. People are now saying he is chosen by God, or the gods, or providence, depending on their beliefs.

Tonight he made a televised speech about a dream he had, when the virus was at its worst...a dream where someone sang to him about the legend of a king and a roofing tile. That is to say, in the dream he was a king of some sort, richly clad, and sitting in a beautifully decorated hall...but a singer was singing him the legend of *another* king, who lived a lot earlier. This earlier king had been warned by an oracle that his great task in life was to fight against an *Iron Empire*. He wasn't fazed by this however, as in his heart it coincided with his own more selfish goal – creating an empire of his own.

So he invaded the lands of this Iron Empire, taking a couple dozen war elephants along with his massive army (and this led Scar-Lo, in the dream, to suspect it was *Hannibal* being sung about...but, as if in response, the singer stressed that this was a full generation before Hannibal was even born).

Then the king offered the Iron Empire peace terms, but they were rejected...so the cup of peace rose in the air and was spilled, and the Moon State then abandoned their own alliance-negotiations with him because his empire-ambitions would bar them from gaining land of their own. And then, the fought-over Lands themselves started to rebel against him, so he had to resort to force and dictatorship to keep them in line. These heavy-handed measures proved so unpopular that the Lands turned against him even more, so that his sun was in eclipse and battles not going his way. Then, after a final struggle he withdrew from the Lands forever, leaving them for the Moon State and the Iron Empire to squabble over.

But his own dreams of empire wouldn't fade, so he turned to another land – the Rugged Peninsula – which he tried to win control of. But resistance was unexpectedly stong, and his own son died in the retreat. Then voices warned him to flee to the woods, but instead of listening to them he chose to interfere in the quarrel of an ancient city that had nothing to do with him. And while he was there, some decrepit crone threw a roofing tile at his head, knocking him down, and a solider finished him off from behind, beheading him.

On waking, Scar-Lo immediately realized that the king in question was some guy called *Pyrrhus of Epirus*.

"Was that who I was?" he asked his viewing audience. "Once I was told (if you believe in such things) that I was the reincarnation of a powerful leader from the past. And now I believe that it must have been Pyrrhus. The Iron Empire, of course, being Rome.

"So I have made a cursory study of Pyrrhus' weaknesses, in order to avoid them myself. His main shortcoming was his tendency to spread his battles too wide, and a failure to band with his enemies against the Iron Empire. For instance, he should have worked harder to cultivate an alliance with the Moon State.

"I swear that I will work harder on my own alliances from henceforth…and if I fall, it will not be from hubris.

"Pyrrhus also had money problems because of his habit of hiring expensive mercenaries, and this, again, is

---

something I can relate to. So I am now calling on all idealists to flock to my banner for nominal wages, in order to build a better world…"

So, now the International Brigade is being flooded with applications – including the Dreamers and Poets, of course, for many artists are fascinated by Scar-Lo's Dream Speech.

The Curia, on the other hand, are using the the speech to convince people that he's insane. They have even announced that the Crusade Against Wahhabism is no longer important, and that the only thing that matters is Scar-lo's standing down and trial for Global Treason…

[…]

A lot has happened since the last time I picked this journal up.

Civil War has come to America, and much of the country is back under Presidential control, but the Nor'westers have seized some big tracts of land in Washington and Idaho (though not as much as they expected, apparently). I have witnessed things that would have made my hair turn grey if it wasn't already dyed green, and I can hear my mother moaning and cursing the fact that she has lived to see such times. Grandma is more cynical, taking it in her stride, just as I would have expected.

Around ten minutes after learning from the TV news about the Civil War, I heard actual shots fired, and later that night we witnessed Presidential soldiers, then Nor'westers, driving through the streets of Aberdeen in open-topped cars. I was stoned, which made it worse, so that it seemed like the cars were the ones in charge…their headlights were cold, mean eyes, and the drivers were their helpless slaves. And they were all going off to a big battle somewhere near Kurt's bridge.

Mom and Grandma were both drunk and arguing about some trivial thing from ten years back, so I went down to the basement and smoked another joint. Then I stretched my limbs and contemplated what the hell I would do if either side won. The alternative, of course, would be a draw, in which Aberdeen would be utterly annihilated. Would Kurt have liked that? Would it be *his* revenge, like Frances Farmer's on Seattle?

The Presidentials will surely win, though, I thought, because they have more troops and resources.

But then, the Nor'westers are more tenacious because they are fighting for an ideal.

I wished, and not for the first time, that *I* had an ideal, too…but all I could see in front of me was the face of Naomi. And with Olympia probably still under Presidential control, she must be in hell tonight, writhing under the jackboot of the enemy.

That thought surprised me…what was lurking in my unconscious, that I would so readily think of Presidentials as 'the enemy'? Wasn't I always raised to think of *Neo-Nazis* as a menace? And the Nor'westers will probably crack down on marijuana if they ever take over, making my own life emptier than ever…

I had a sudden vision of them, these Nor'westers…grim-faced elementals, men of wrath, all lined up like square-jawed mannikins, staring with hard contempt at the decadent liberals of Cascadia, of whom they would certainly number myself as one. Laser beams would shoot from their eyes, obliterating us all, making a dirt patch in which they could grow corn and start from scratch, or something, with all decadence erased. Hey, that might be the best solution. Isn't decadence the root cause of depression – the depression that afflicts so many of us around here – and isn't depression a sign of unworthiness? And isn't unworthiness another word for *unworth?*

So come on, men of oak, blow us all away!

But fuck, fuck, fuck, something in me wants to keep living…

And again, I see Naomi's face before me, stretching out into the far distance.

[…]

The guns are tapping out their autistic messages again…but why do I get the strong feeling that the Nor'westers have won?

[…]

It's confirmed: the North West Front has taken Aberdeen and Hoquiam, while Olympia and the Seattle region remain under Presidential control.

So I'm cut off from Naomi, probably for good.

[…]

The square-jawed mannikins have taken over, and they have been ruling Aberdeen better than people would have thought. They have acted to stimulate independent trade and bartering, and have also set up a simple welfare system for those who have lost their livelihoods due to the war (which is quite a lot of people). My family is scraping by okay, but I have been drafted for the town labor brigade, and have to spend six hours a day, five days a week repairing damage from the Battle of Aberdeen. Other than that, my time is my own. It's not so bad…

One thing that will *not* be fixed is the varied assortment of Cobain statues – in fact we have been tasked with pulling them down. One of the first acts of the Nor'westers was to abolish Cobain Day, which wasn't much of an issue with the populace, although not everyone is happy about its replacement holiday – Hitler's Birthday. But we all get double rations on Führertag, whereas all we got on Cobain Day was the right to smoke weed in public, and a general feeling of malaise.

The colored (Black and Hispanic) population has been transferred to the Presidential territories in exchange for certain square-jawed prisoners held in internment camps near Seattle. I thought this would raise some protests, but no one seems to care, except for my mother who mutters harsh words over it.

I find myself constantly wondering what Naomi is doing. Is she humming a Nirvana song and waiting for better times? Has she found a sweetheart, or perhaps gotten engaged? I'll probably never know. She stopped emailing anyone I know in Aberdeen ages ago, and it's now illegal to send emails to Presidential territory (though they have no way of policing it). I don't know her email address anyway, and even if I did, you need some kind of special dongle to get the internet now, which we don't have and can't afford.

The Nor'westers seem serious about moving to a barter economy, though it's being done in dribs and drabs and I'm not sure how long it will be before the money stashed under Grandma's mattress is declared worthless. Oh well, we struggle on.

Scar-Lo himself has been to Aberdeen!

He was invited as a guest by several of the patchwork of mini-states that constitute the North West Republic, and though he declined the honorary presidency, he chose to accept the invitation to visit. And by doing so he has apparently earned further pariah status as a 'Nazi' by the 'international community' (i.e. the Curia-controlled media), who have declared him even worse than the elderly Vladimir Putin…but hardly anyone takes the 'international community' seriously any more, and those who do waste their time gossiping in cafes in Seattle or Portland, and aren't much threat to anyone.

I actually attended the speech by Scar-Lo, right near the ruins of my old smoking spot, where the Kurt statue that was never finished has now been carted off to landfill. I wonder if the seagulls still fight over who gets to shit on it?

It was surreal seeing a celebrity in the flesh. I didn't have a very good view, but it was obvious how different Scar-Lo looks in real life than on the TV…more fragile, somehow, as if burdened with the weight of the world…and perhaps he is. There is a flame beneath the surface, however, that aroused my awe and, I'm ashamed to say, my envy. Why does my own flame find it so hard to catch hold and illumine the dazzled shell in which it burns? Are some flames purer than others, or do they burn with a higher heat? I would give anything to know.

Scar-Lo's speech was mainly about autonomy, and gained a rousing reception from the crowd. Everyone who saw it seemed electrified afterwards, though I don't know how long that will last. I have to admit my own feet are kind of skipping…Scar-Lo must have some magical ability, a power to motivate crowds.

He is also very intelligent – much of his speech about economic autarchy and regionalism went completely over my head. But he stated very clearly that while he didn't agree with all the views of the Nor'westers, he now recognizes that they have set up their own state and are creating a unique culture for the non-metropolitan parts of Cascadia.

"The Puget Sound area will remain a Free Port under Presidential control," he roared, "but in the areas outside of it, the North West Republic is here to stay. I recognize it unconditionally, giving it an honored place in my coming Imperium!" There was a wave of raptured cheering and applause…and so I think the residents of Aberdeen have gotten used to the idea that they are part of a new nation. It didn't take them long. American flags have been banned, and many are already flying the North West flag in their front yards, though it isn't required by law. Aberdeeners are adaptable…

But what happens now that Scar-Lo has gone away? Who will motivate us tomorrow? It remains to be seen.

[…]

A talking head, some guy who used to be a 'Catholic traditionalist' but who publicly renounced religion and threw in his lot with the Curia, has declared that the Curia would have *revoked* its fatwa against Scar-Lo if it hadn't been for his diplomatic visit to the North West, which apparently put him beyond the pale.

Malicious bluffing swipe? Would they *really* have rescinded the declaration of heresy?

Then I could have seen Naomi again…

But I doubt it. These people are liars through and through.

So I lit some incense and visualized her instead.

And now Scar-Lo has sent communications to ALL world leaders, asking them to pick sides between him and the Curia.

So that's it.

World War Three is coming.

I have to cross the Great Divide and see her, just once...once would be enough.

I think that Grandma knows how I feel. She hasn't said anything directly (how could she, as she doesn't know specifics), but she talks about roses being the finest flowers because they're harder to pick, and about life being what we make of it. She is encouraging me, despite the danger, or so I choose to think.

Something is awakening inside me. Is it courage?

[...]

Here I am, betraying my new country for the cursed Presidential Territories, all for the love of a girl who probably barely remembers me. I'm a fuck-up, but a happy one at present. If it's all an illusion, then let me enjoy it while it lasts.

Aberdeen to Olympia is fifty miles as the crow flies, and it felt good leaving in the morning before Mom or Grandma were up, after first filling my backpack with food and plucking a flower from next door's garden, knowing that I might never see my hometown again. I couldn't find a rose, so I had to make do with some saggy pink mongrelly weed, with bugs crawling all over it. Then I got a bus to Cosmopolis and started hitchhiking.

The traffic is much thinner than it was before the new Civil War (or 'War Between the Hates' as some wit dubbed it). On the other side of the road some guy was hitching in the opposite direction. There were big gaps in the traffic so we got to talking, and I told him I was seeking love in the east.

"Heading out west myself…"

"How come you don't get the bus through Aberdeen and Hoquiam? There won't be many cars going all the way through."

"Don't have a penny to my name."

"Hardcore! So where are you trying to get to?"

"The sea. I've lived within ninety miles of it my whole life but never seen it. What a joke! World war's on the way, and I have to see the ocean before I die, man. It'll be *immense*." I was silent, not knowing if he meant the ocean, the experience of seeing it, or his impending death. Then a car stopped and picked him up, and it was then that I realized the *only* cars passing were going westwards. Was there some conflict in the borderlands people were fleeing from? Although it is a cliché to gulp nervously, I did so.

But ten minutes later a car finally came the right way, and stopped. The wiry fellow who opened the door had a hardline stare, and his face twitched as if there were strange electric pulses running through his body. He said he was going as far as Porter, some thirty miles down the road.

"Awesome," I said, jumping in. "That gets me most of the way there."

"And where is *there?*" he asked as we screeched away down the road. (I was glad there was so little traffic because his driving was already making me nervous.) I didn't want to say Olympia, so I muttered the name of a town south of Porter, and he laughed.

"You can't fool me. I know you're headed into the Hodgelands."

"No, no…"

"Yes, yes. It's written all over you. Soft little lank like

you couldn't hack it in a White Republic. Oh don't worry, I won't tell. I ain't on anyone's side. I'm just a mercenary. I kill for *money*. Principles can fuck themselves, har har har." (I can't write his laugh down properly, it was a kind of gargling growl).

Well, I won't lie, I was starting to get a bit scared. Historically there have been a lot of serial killers in this area, like Billy Gohl, and the Green River Killer, and this guy seemed like he would fit their ranks well. Then he said: "Take a look in the glove compartment." I did so, and saw a pistol with a silencer which looked suspiciously like a replica, but as I know shit all about guns I couldn't be sure, so I shut the compartment nervously.

"The Silent Killer they call me," he leered. "I take out who I want to take out, Presidential or Nor'wester. But don't worry, pal, I won't kill you. You're too soft-looking to be worth it. Bet you're one of those crinkly-eyed potheads, ain't that right?" He seemed certain, so there was no point arguing. I merely gave a nervous laugh.

"Course you are," he said with condescending pity. And then, true to his name, the Silent Killer passed the rest of the journey in complete silence, the better to hear my heart beating with fear over the engine noise.

I was ready to grab the gun at any moment, just in case he tried reaching for it, but to my relief he was true to his word, and dropped me outside of Porter, giving a sardonic salute by way of farewell. I sucked the oxygen in deeply and gratefully.

After walking a couple of miles down some backroads, I found myself in the Capitol State Forest, a big tract of woodland with four-wheel-drive tracks and hiking trails running through it.

I trudged through the forest for at least two hours without coming across a single soul. Then, during a rest on a tree stump to eat, I heard the sound of female sobbing in the distance, and had a sudden vision of

Naomi, so I walked cautiously towards it. A girl around my own age was sitting on a mossy log and blubbing, a bottle of cheap wine her only companion. I approached deferentially, and asked timidly what the matter was.

"I'm crying because Jake, m-my boyfriend, is in Olympia. We're separated *forever*. And I've vowed to pine away near the border."

"Well, I'm going to Olympia myself, to see my…uh, a girl I know. So maybe we could go there together."

"No…like I said…I've vowed to pine away."

"Oh."

There wasn't much else to say after that, so I went on my way through the forest. She seemed taken aback as I walked off, but aside from an intensification of her blubbing, said nothing.

Should I have handled the situation differently? I'm not sure what I was supposed to have done…I was hardly going to throw my arms around her neck and implore her, was I?

Anyway, in the late afternoon, I finally began to approach the borderlands. I paused to look at the handdrawn map I had copied from a real one in the library, and as I stood there trying to make head or tail of it, afternoon gradually turned into twilight. I decided on a path, and after walking for fifteen minutes I stumbled on a cache of abandoned logging equipment on which two weird children were playing a game that seemed to invoke the souls of the dead.

"Three nights spent in the house of death," they chanted. "To tame wild wisdom's breath…"

And then a ragged old man, apparently their grandfather emerged from a nearby shack, and asked who I was. My instinct told me to trust him, so I said I was trying to get across the border to Olympia (but not the reason why). It turned out he was a *smuggler*, and offered to take me across with his run of goods that very night! I was in luck.

The goods, it turned out, consisted of packages of compressed marijuana. I asked how many times he had done the smuggling run, and it turned out this was the first time! Still, he seemed like he knew what he was doing.

Our adventure took us four or five miles through the moonlit woods. At one point we came across a female trapper, who turned out to be a Nor'wester setting traps for enemy soldiers (they were old-fashioned steel raccoon traps).

"And what if you get one of our own by mistake?" asked Gramps.

"Then I'll drag him back to the bedroom," she grinned, "and have some fun while I heal his mangled foot."

For some reason I thought she said 'heel' his mangled foot, and that her traps were therefore particularly vicious. Even after realizing I had misinterpreted, I noticed that she had a slightly sadistic leer about her, so I kept walking, and Gramps soon followed. She didn't twig to the possibility we might have been smugglers.

The next folks we came across were from the Presidential side, and it now became clear that the old man had made previous arrangements to bribe them (presidential troops being notoriously corrupt, unlike the NWers). And to cut a long story short, we got through. I farewelled Gramps and made my way towards the city of destiny.

So that was the story of my adventures in no-man's land. Now it's dawn, and I'm lying by a muddy stream outside Olympia, hiding from patrols, with freezing northwest rain coming down on the back of my neck like tiny heroin needles. So here's a big hearty 'fuck you', Kurt, from the muddy banks of an unnamed creek (not the pathetic Wishkah). You had nothing to whine about, but I expect your ghost has faded by now…there are other spirits on the march.

[…]

Well, I managed to penetrate Olympia without anyone asking me for papers. The city is almost free of soldiers, because they've all been dispatched to the borderlands. Even so, it seems like a place of faded glory. The student types seemed even more sedate than usual, as if struck by the fact that everything they believed in the past has now been invalidated.

I walked past the hostel on the way to the campus, and it was shut down. Not surprising, really, as these aren't exactly prime tourist years that we're living through. But *I* felt like I was in Paris in the Spring, and my heart was beating rapturously.

I strolled down the Evergreen Parkway and finally arrived at the campus. There was no extra security as I had feared, but glossy flyers were posted everywhere, with messages like:

SEE SOMETHING, SAY SOMETHING: REPORT ANY *SEPARATIST* TALK ON CAMPUS.

Another one said:

ANTI-GLOBAL SPEECH IS NOT FREE SPEECH.

And my favourite:

MOCKING YOUR ELECTED REPRESENTATIVES HELPS THE ENEMY.

The word 'enemy' had blood dripping from its letters. At least the no-nonsense Nazis in Aberdeen don't resort to that kind of cheese…

I now reached the gleaming new student dormitory building, and milled around until someone came out of an electronically locked door, passing in quickly as he did so. Then I sat still as a mouse on a sofa in the foyer, wondering what to do. Should I knock on every damned door? There must be hundreds of dorms in this massive building.

I got up intending to do so, and then...I saw her. She entered the foyer with a tall black guy and a couple of skinny white chicks. She was looking very skinny herself...the campus diet, no doubt. I walked across to her.

She glanced at me with a kind of tired sneer...then looking more closely, her eyes narrowed with confusion.

"*Harlan?*"

"Yep."

"Are you at college now?"

"Nope."

"Then what are you doing here?"

"Uh..." I glanced at the black guy, who was doing his best to give a 'I be wise patriarchal nigga, you want me deal with this skinny white dweeb?' kind of look, but thankfully she said: "I'll catch you guys up." She was probably embarrassed they had to see me at all. The football scholar nodded, and sauntered out the door, his two 'bitches' giving me curious looks on the way out.

Naomi said in a cold voice: "Well, do you want to come up to my dorm and explain things?"

"All right."

A plush elevator, then a walk past a lot of doors, and we were in the room that she shared with another girl, who fortunately wasn't there, discussing things. But I couldn't melt the frost from her voice, no matter how hard I tried.

"You mean you crossed the border *illegally?*" Her eyes bulged out. "You fucking *idiot* Harlan. It's lucky I've known you so long, or I'd report you to the authorities, for sure."

Even as she said it, I noticed a poster above her bed with two crying children under a Mexican flag…the poster said 'No one is illegal.' And on her chest of drawers was a sticker celebrating 'Open Borders Day' (which fell near to the Hoquiam Cobain Day). But although Naomi has turned into a hypocrite, I felt I could still save her. After looking round at the photos on the wall, which were mainly of her in compromising positions with people of both sexes, I turned to her and said: "I love you."

She gave me a look of what can only be described as murderous hatred. For a moment I thought she was going to call campus security, but then she took cold pity on me.

"Go back to Aberdeen, Harlan. We don't want dreamers here. Look at the trouble they cause – look at Maximillian Scarlotti."

"Wasn't *Kurt* a dreamer?"

"I'm not a fan of Kurt's…I'm no longer writing my thesis on him."

"Why?"

"He liked guns too much. It didn't sit right with me as a gun control advocate."

So, she had become a true conformist, one of the dreaded campus normals!

"But you already *knew* he liked guns."

"It came to overshadow his more progressive qualities for me…there was a point when it became too much. *He wasn't the person that I needed him to be.*"

I felt a sudden flash of rage, against her and against Kurt, and I believe I began yelling incoherently. Then Naomi said calmly but firmly: "If you stay, I'll have to report you." So I left, and found this little closet at the end of the hallway to write my diary and to let off steam.

What the fuck did I come here for? This icy bitch who looks at me with the eyes of an enemy? How could *this* have been the girl I had fixed in my mind for so long?

She isn't, of course, *but where did that girl go?*

And now I have a vision, for the first time in months, of how my twin sister died.

I was five years old, sick with an infectious illness. Mom still lived with my drunken father at the time, and Grandma offered to take my sister back to her place so she didn't get sick also. But on the way there was a car crash…which Grandma survived and my sister didn't.

And Mom still blames me for killing her, because *I* was the one who got sick.

Oh shit, now there are footsteps outside the door.

Cobain, it is *you* Naomi has betrayed.


*[Coad was taken to an internment camp near Bremerton, WA, and terminated by lethal injection for wartime espionage. – E.J.C.]*

6

## THE TESTIMONY OF
## DR. ADRIAN SAVAGE

Rendering this report in plain language (avoiding psychiatric jargon as much as possible) should be relatively easy, as existing medical terms are completely useless when describing Johnny 'Buffo' Stokes, who, psychiatrically speaking, is a law unto himself.

Of course, I understand your distrust of headshrinkers and their jargon. There are more psychiatrists than ever in the military at this point. Many of the 'mental health community' found themselves out of work after Scarface's selective editing of the forces, but under Presidential rule they have been reinstated and reinforced. Not that this was entirely unwarranted – there is an increasingly fine line between the soldier given leeway to kill and the soldier who is court-martialled or put in a loony bin *for killing*, and the stress for grunts who constantly make these kind of calls is enormous (though this may change with the gathering intensity of the war against Scarface, where, I predict, increasingly, anything will go), and then, of course, there are the psychiatrists needed for the *children* of the military – lots and lots of them.

So with our numbers swollen like never before, it should perhaps come as no surprise that an anti-psychiatric movement has emerged in the forces. One of its founding members (who blew his own brains out after the First Battle of Damascus) even had a slogan: 'mental illness is a myth'. Now that's going *too* far...

Anyway, back to the report. I was assigned to Buffo as part of my research fellowship, sponsored by the The Reverend Dr. Martin Luther King, Jr. Institute for Psychiatric Medicine. The topic of my research was, and still is, the problem of difficult-to-diagnose battlefield trauma, and Buffo seemed a case in point.

The shrink originally assigned to his case made a cursory diagnosis of symphorophilia (a condition whereby sexual arousal is achieved by witnessing disasters, in this case the carnage of war). But this proved not to be the case at all – the cause of Buffo's agitation not being sexual in nature, at least not *directly* so. Nor do I believe it to be any kind of PTSD. I can only report what I have observed at first hand. His condition is truly a mysterious one.

On first landing in the Middle East I reported to a Combat Stress Control unit on board the non-comissioned hospital ship USNS The Reverend Dr. Martin Luther King, Jr., where Buffo had been brought for an evaluation before being released back into active duty (he was too valuable to spare for long, even with his curious condition). I was briefed on board ship, then flown into the combat zone to begin my fellowship. From that point, I was on my own.

I found Buffo in an urban part of the southern Iraqi war zone at the break of dawn, heading off for a morning snipe. Snipers usually work in two-man teams, with a shooter and spotter taking turns to avoid eye fatigue, but Buffo didn't need a spotter or flanker...he had eyes of steel.

While Buffo was the PS military's best sniper by far, beating Chris Kyle's record (with over 240 confirmed kills), his mental instability had become the subject of concern. Any other soldier with his stress levels would have been relieved from active duty, but, as I said, Buffo was too valuable to spare. And while emotionally troubled soldiers can endanger the mission, that wasn't what bothered Buffo's superiors…the fact is, they were concerned about the possibility of him defecting to the other side.

So I approached him, still considering how to initiate conversation. What would be his attitude to having a shrink attached to him for large parts of his day?

As it turned out, I needn't have worried. He seemed eager to welcome me, shaking hands vigorously when I told him who I was.

"I fucking hate sand niggers," he grinned (those were his exact first words to me), "but I *love* homosexuals. If you're gay, then you're alright with me."

"I'm not…gay…actually."

"Oh. Are you some other kind of LGBTTQQIAAPCINDNQQINBTSAO?" (He had actually memorized this now outmoded and faintly non-PC acronym, pronouncing it clearly and distinctly for my benefit).

"No."

"But…you're *tolerant*, right?"

"Well, sure…I like to think of myself as a tolerant person."

"Alright, doc, that's just as well. If there's one thing I can't stand it's homophobes. Now sand niggers…" He stared off in the distance, as if scouring for the enemy.

"Yes?"

"They should all just die. Because they hate faggots. Gays, I mean. I wish I was gay myself, but unfortunately I like women too much, ha ha." As he said it, I was reminded of that unfortunate historical figure Kurdt Kobain, who had also apparently wished himself to be homosexual. I didn't bother telling Buffo that the term 'gay' had been banished from progressive circles for quite some time, and was now considered as quaint and patronizing as 'negro' once had been, before it was replaced by 'black', then 'POC', then 'nigga', then 'negar', then 'blackamore'. (And recently, of course, 'negro' has again become the sole polite term.)

But although Buffo was uneducated, and could not be expected to keep up with such limber subtleties, in his own way he had a flexible mind...although I could sense, too, a certain level of aggression inside him, and steeled myself in case it should come to the surface. Typically, solider stress occurs due to easily understandable factors – combat fatigue, or a 'Dear John' letter from a girlfriend. Buffo's stress, on the other hand (and it was palpable), had a completely unknown cause. I was determined to get to the bottom of it, although I realized I would have to take things at a relaxed pace, approaching the matter subtly over the course of several weeks or months.

While Buffo's love of all things 'LGBTTQQIAAPCINDNQQINBTSAO' at least demonstrated a patriotic loyalty to the values of the Presidential States (so much that I wondered if his superiors might have jumped the gun somewhat in fearing he would defect), I couldn't deny that there was a paradox at the heart of his persona that I had yet to get to grips with.

Well, after some more conversation on the topic of 'sand niggers', he bade me follow as he went to set up his sniping post, and we entered a house in darkness. I sat quietly in a dark corner while he arranged things (avoiding being sighted is a real skill, as you can imagine). In the dust of the clay shelves in my desolate corner I imagined I could see the remnants of the countless races and civilizations inhabiting this fruitless and eternally fought-over part of the world, this land between two rivers. Then, as Buffo adjusted a curtain, I had a strange vision in the sudden sunlight that I could see dawn coming...or was it actually sunset? Everything seemed red, murky, ominous.

"Scarface's supposed to be arriving in this part of the warzone soon," Buffo growled, keeping his voice low. "I can't wait to have a crack at him." I said nothing, doubting he would get the chance. Security would be intense – the leader of the reactionary world had already been hit by stray shrapnel soon after his arrival in the warzone, thus earning (from progressive troops) his nickname of 'Scarface'.

Scarface has been smeared massively by our propagandists, who claim that he rapes and beats his wife, and worse things. And Buffo eagerly joined in the smears, adding that Scarface was a 'homophobe,' who deserved to die a slow death because of that. I thought I would use the opportunity to subtly probe the sniper on his knowledge of world events.

"So, I hear Scarface is supposed to have fallen out somewhat with Mohammed Tate," I casually remarked.

"Ah, they're all cut from the same raghead cloth," muttered Buffo as he 'zeroed in' his weapon (military jargon for the process of adjusting his weapon's scope for accuracy at a specific distance).

"Well, yes, they're still fighting on the same side, no matter what their personal differences may be," I admitted. "And our side can certainly learn something from that kind of pragmatic approach."

"The only thing I learn from homophobic sand niggers is *shooting skills*," grinned Buffo. "Moving targets are always the most educative."

I nodded, not wanting to antagonize him. His anti-Islam sentiments were somewhat misplaced, however – the Curia cared not a whit now for their former anti-jihadist crusade, their sole focus being on killing Scarface. Perhaps they had even tried to bribe Emir Tate, but for now, at least, he was still nominally on his son-in-law's side. It was rumored, too, that the Curia were going to launch a concentrated attack on America's 'North-West Republic', though this had yet to be confirmed.

But none of these delicate issues clouded the mind of Johnny 'Buffo' Stokes. He continued to set up his nest, putting a finger outside the window to determine the wind velocity, air temperature and humidity. He was certainly an expert at his job. I attempted once more to engage him in conversation, remarking briefly on the decentralized nature of fourth generation warfare, and the complex, shifting alliances between the clans of the local area (having been briefed on this at the hospital ship), noting possible similarities to the famous Iron Age battle in which Pyrrhus of Epirus had died.

"Better get your roofing tiles ready, then," chuckled Buffo. So, he was familiar with Scarface's famous 'Dream Speech' at least, and thus not completely ignorant of world affairs. From that point on he would refer to his sniping bullets as 'roofing tiles', and then 'rofling tiles' (as he would be rolling on the floor laughing when he finally killed Scarface, he said).

Before I could make further conversation, there was a flurry at the door, and we both wheeled round in alarm, Buffo reaching for his rifle. It turned out to be a false alarm, though – a camera crew had burst in on us.

I imagined Buffo would be incensed, but he merely demanded to know if the crew were homophobes. When they assured him they weren't, he proceeded to grant them an interview, on the sole condition it would not be broadcast for twenty-four hours, thus preserving the location of his current sniper's nest. A live interview, of course, might give his position away to the enemy. (Something that really irritates me about the current war is the constant presence of the media. I have personally witnessed an armored camera crew running alongside soldiers and insurgents during a pitched street battle, and boy did they look ludicrous. I even heard of an actual firefight between rival camera crews in a different part of the warzone.)

I chatted briefly with the camera crew about the terrorism, not officially sanctioned by either side but an increasingly common phenomenon among civilian combatants (car bombs being a lot cheaper than standard military equipment). As for the official troops, in general they fight with much the same weapons as in previous Middle Eastern wars, with the much-vaunted sound weapons and EMP (electromagnetic pulse) tech still at the experimental stage, and not likely to put in an appearance on the battlefield anytime soon.

I learnt little that was concrete from Buffo on the first snipe, however, as his chatter to the journalists consisted entirely of various inanities, and I felt that if I made any inroads at all into his character, they would be slow ones. Only the coming days would tell if I could forge real tracks.

Next day came news, however.

He of the shrapnel-ravaged visage had arrived in our part of the warzone, as part of a greater tour giving motivational speeches to his troops. Buffo was like a child at Christmas, bouncing around so much that I thought he would piss his pants. When he finally managed to utter a coherent sentence, he confessed himself *desperate* to be the one to put a bullet into Scarface. I told him not to submit to false hopes, as his nemesis was likely to be surrounded by vast cordons of security, but Buffo ignored me, rocking back and forth with glee.

That night I had an interview with his immediate superior, Lieutenant Jonathan Briggs, who I tackled on Buffo's chronic Islamophobia (a court-martial offence, incidentally, which in his case was overlooked by an army desperate to keep such a lucky-charm killing machine within its ranks). Apparently this was the cause of friction with some of the other troops, who were themselves strictly gagged from expressing similar sentiment about the Religion of Peace (in fact, the very term 'Religion of Peace' has recently been banned by the military, due to the fact that some incorrigible rogues had been known to utter it sarcastically.)

Briggs was a soft-spoken man, and shook his head sadly as he told me that Buffo not only *denied* being Islamophobic, but had once had said (in the same breath as expressing a wish to "exterminate all Muslims") that he "will *kill* anyone who thinks that I'm Islamophobic." This kind of doublethink is marvellous to contemplate, only adding to the depths of Buffo's mystery.

Two days later, he walked up with a gleam in his eye and beckoned me aside, confiding that representatives of the Curia had just approached him brazenly inside the warzone (above his superiors' heads), and asked him to undertake the very sniping mission he had so longed for – his target being Scarface himself.

"They showed accreditation," he said, "so I know these boys are genuine." I couldn't be sure that he was telling the truth, but played along to keep him onside.

"That's great," I said. "And when will you carry out the mission?"

"Right now," he said. "They've told me about a farm house where I can get a clear shot at the place Scarface will be at eighteen hundred Juliett, this very evening, do you understand? I'm gonna be the most famous goddamn sniper in history!" I heartily congratulated him, wondering if perhaps the Curia really *had* approached him. He then made it clear that he wanted me to accompany him, as a witness to the mission. Under the terms of my fellowship, I could hardly refuse.

We were provided with a detachment to secure the building, indicating that there *were* higher-ups involved, and that afternoon, to cut a long story short, I found myself crouching on the dirt floor of a decrepit outbuilding, on an ancient wheat farm that had somehow survived all the various Iraq conflicts, waiting for Buffo to take a plug at Scarface. A successful shot could win the entire war, since it was only Scarface's organizational genius that allowed the disparate anti-Curia forces to unite and gain the upper hand.

The tension was unbearable, and our eyes were drawn irresistably to Buffo's eye, glued to the scope of his M2024 rifle. He would only get one shot; there was no possibility of relocation. If Scarface occupied the position he was meant to, then that shot would be just under a mile, and as Buffo had made over thirty of his kills from further distances than that, he was certainly in with a chance. But his bullet would be in the air for nearly four seconds before finding its target, losing much of its kinetic energy on the way, and many things could happen in that time. Scarface might move in an unexpected direction, or a cross-breeze could divert the bullet from its trajectory. And although the air was still and sultry, there were untold dust-motes in these camel lands, making zeroing harder to achieve.

Then, at last, the moment came.

"I can *see* that sumbitch," Buffo murmured, "so it's now or never."

He squeezed the trigger almost sexually. The four seconds of tension felt like four long minutes…and then he let out a groan of scorched despair, deeper than I have ever known human tongue to utter.

"And why did he wanna move *that* way for?" he sobbed uncontrollably. "What in the blue hell did I do to *deserve* it?"

Things sure were glum around the base that night. I visited Buffo in his tent, and on entering heard him mutter something about "killing homos"…but I must have misheard him…"killing homophobes," it most likely was. In any case, he had taken his failure to heart, and now seemed to think that Scarface was operating under some kind of divine protection.

"Is *God* a homophobe?" he asked me in all seriousness, and when I failed to answer he began to mutter curses, at one point expressing a wish to snipe the Almighty. He was slowly becoming more crazy-eyed, and his circling movements began to remind me of a cat chasing its own tail.

I assured him anyone could have missed the shot at such a distance, with a four second gap between firing and striking, but he wouldn't listen to my reasoning so I decided to let him be. There wasn't any point in increasing his agitation.

But he didn't want me to leave. He swung round and grabbed me by the collar, his moon-face grinning ineffably into mine. One second it seemed there was a great mystery behind his countenance, the next I felt sure I was gazing into a void – empty tiger-like teeth hanging meaningless in mid-air, covered in blood-flecked spittle, concealing nothing underneath.

Which glance was right?

"All right, Buffo, it's been a long day," I said, "and I'm going to go get some sleep now, okay? We can talk further in the morning." Slowly, as if engaged in a pointless ritual, he released his grip on my shirt and gave a weird sigh.

"I thought I saw you falling, Doc," he said in a tired voice. "Today, I thought I saw you falling and you couldn't get up. I kind of wanted to help you, but couldn't. I don't rightly know *what* was happening."

Needless to say, I hadn't fallen that day, and Buffo was now beginning to officially freak me out. Professional as I was, I thought it best to depart his tent without further talk, in the hope that he would be less disturbed in the morning.

I slept uneasily, waking half a dozen times with

lukewarm fragments of dreams crawling behind my eyeballs. In one of these, I dreamt I was asleep and couldn't wake myself up…I was yelling really loud, but couldn't get myself to hear.

In the morning, I began to ask myself just what the hell I was doing in Mesopotamia.

The afternoon brought further news, however…after the latest attempt on his life, our intelligence services had learnt that Scarface had now flown to the opposite side of the current theater of war – to Syria, heart of the Provisional Emirate, no doubt to meet with his father-in-law, Tate, to further discuss their differences. And it looked as if Buffo was going to be flown there, too, to have another shot at the bigtime, and naturally I would be obliged to accompany him.

So we left next morning. On the flight, I had a disturbing vision of my patient as a Little Lost Lamb who just wanted to be loved, but this was swiftly replaced by the sight of his hands stained purple with blood, and I started to wonder if my own sanity was slipping. I couldn't worry about such things, though…I had a job to do.

It was several miles above the desert that we first heard news of attacks by combined Curia armies on the nascent North West Republic in America (and Buffo muttered something like "Good riddance, homophobic *freaks*"). Then there was another message – insurgents had just killed Dano DeLacey, the world's most famous transexual solider. This predictably sent Buffo into conniptions. He turned to the nearest person, a lieutenant of Arab extraction, and started on a rant about "goddamned dune coons…can you believe it, sir?" (The Arab lieutenant nodded sympathetically.) This proved to me beyond all doubt that "sand nigger" for Buffo was a mere abstraction, not a term of actual racial vilification. Good, I was making progress…

The steward brought us trays of roasted chestnuts, which I thought was an odd thing to serve on a flight, and I tuned my headset to the announcements (on every channel) that DeLacey's funeral would be shown live on all networks in America...but that furious arguments had broken out between varying factions of transexuals, feminists, anti-militarists etc. as to the significance of the event. I asked Buffo where he stood on these issues, and he became confused. I noticed the empty look in his eyes again, and so changed the subject.

Then the plane descended. There was a dazzle from the tarmac, so that it seemed we were entering some shimmering hell, and my head began throbbing with a persistence scarcely to be endured. I clenched my teeth, determined to present a face of complete normalcy, although my tongue felt like it was coated with a silvery substance like mercury, and my innards performed a twisting dance of slow strangulation. I hobbled downstairs onto the tarmac, and slumped into the waiting jeep with something resembling gratitude.

We were ushered into a small field office, whose atrium was covered with pictures of homosexual couples kissing and fondling, and notices saying it was a court martial offence to remove or deface them. I was shown to a small room, where I lay down to take a quick nap, hoping I would feel better on waking. But just as I was fuzzing off into dreamland there was a knock at the door, pushing electric barbs into the backs of my eyes. It was Buffo.

"I'm going on a mission now, doc," he said. "Thought you might like to know."

"Of course. I'll come along. Just let me get dressed, and splash some water over my face."

"As you wish, doc."

But when I finished, he was nowhere to be seen. A search of the field office and surrounds revealed no trace, and I went back to my room, scratching my head with puzzlement, and for other reasons.

An hour later, I learnt he had gone out *sans permisson*, to try to snipe a unit said to be directly from the fief of Mohammed Tate. The latter, though white as the driven snow, was an arch "dune coon" to Buffo, confirming my tentative view that my patient was a mere solipsist…but that would be too easy a diagnosis, I thought, and surely not worth an entire fellowship.

I waited for further news of Buffo, mulling over the possibility that the Curia had approached him again in secret with a new location for Scarface.

I read up online about the latter's father-in-law, who had started out as a semi-romantic Turpin-like camel thief, but who in the chaotic last days of ISIS had emerged as a powerful warlord, and eventually the emir of a secular provisional state, which despite (or because of) occasional heavy-handedness, had been greeted with immense relief by the ISIS-ravaged denizens of Syria and northern Iraq. Initially the Curia, for whom ISIS had become a liablity, had welcomed Tate's rule, but they soon turned against him when he revealed himself as disturbingly competent and efficient. And now it looks as if our side's strategy is to try and drive a wedge between Tate and his volatile son-in-law…but so far this has not been a success, for there is every sign they will be reconciled, and even their present rift has not hampered a united war effort.

I stood and looked at the little bouncy Syrian clouds, wondering idly if someone like Buffo was, after all, for the best in the best of all possible worlds…and then dismissed the idea as supremely ridiculous.

A sergeant approached and informed me that a detachment had been formed for the purpose of locating Buffo, and (for reasons still unknown to me) I immediately volunteered to be attached to the unit. After

---

some initial hesitation I was given the green light to go with them, possibly into a combat zone. I should have been greatly afraid, but in fact I felt calm, even confident. My presence would give the mission a touch of class, I foolishly thought.

We sailed out like Argonauts into Syrian dirt, and I listened idly to the talk of the troops as our jeeps bumped along...it seemed that they had mixed feelings at best about the famous sniper, and not a few jokes were made at his expense – including malicious ones. But what did that matter to me? My job was to analyse Buffo's mind, not to assess his popularity.

Then, after twenty minutes or so, we entered al-B___, a smallish town, where we left our jeeps under guard while we combed the place on foot. There had been insurgent activity here in the last week by jihadi rebels (sworn enemies of both ourselves and Tate). Mere amateurs compared to the ISIS of old, of course, but still potentially dangerous. And, what do you know, as we neared the far end of town, a dozen or so men with black masks, wielding submachine guns, turned the corner, coming face to face with their American enemies. There was a standoff, both our commander and theirs seemingly frozen and unsure of what to do.

Just as the situation seemed to be devolving into stalemate, however, something unexpected happened – a platoon of Tate's troops entered from another branch of the intersection. They weren't even supposed to be in this area. Now we were caught between the devil and the deep blue sea...

The spell was immediately broken, and a three-way fire-fight ensued. Despite being armed, my first act was to dive into a pile of rubble, avoiding the bullets that were flying in every possible direction. After cowering in the rubble for what may have been ten seconds (but felt like a lot longer), I suddenly heard a familiar and greatly-loathed voice.

"Doc," it hissed. "Get out of my line of fire, damn it!" And an arm reached through a window and pulled me back into a semi-ruined building. It was Buffo, of course, and he was far from pleased to see me.

"I had everything under control," he growled, "until you clowns made an appearance. I had a clear shot at Hani Fakhoury, who's an important commander in Tate's army."

But even as he scolded me there was a deep booming blast outside, and the walls of the building seemed to collapse around us. I huddled on the floor, losing consciousness. When I came to, it was in a strangely darkened room.

"Where are the lights?" I muttered.

"It's getting on towards evening, doc," came the voice, "and not much light gets in through the airhole."

"Airhole?"

"Yeah, that's right…we're trapped in here, in case you didn't notice. But don't you worry. There's a tiny shaft in the rubble where the air gets through."

"My god…what will happen to us?"

"I don't rightly know."

"Are you *sure* we're completely trapped?"

"Course I'm sure." He sounded mildly offended. "I've checked throughly. Someone heard me yelling though the airhole, though…so if our boys capture the town, someone'll *prolly* see fit to rescue us. But if the sand monkeys take it, well…"

I suddenly became dizzy, and he passed me a large flask.

"Go easy on the water, doc. It's all we got. And dark's closing in. If we're rescued it won't be til morning, so ease up. Don't chug so, damn it. What're you so nervous of?"

How could I tell him that night was falling, night was falling? The ruined walls seemed to close in around me,

99

and I put my face to the airhole, sucking the dusty air which felt infinitely cleaner than the miasma surrounding Buffo in the claustrophobic gloom.

"Don't you have a light?" I muttered. "Don't soldiers carry torches?"

He giggled. "No torches, doc. No light tonight." It was a new moon, too, I thought with a shudder. A wave of cold seemed to billow up from the floor. I was in my tomb, it seemed, my very own precious tomb, and there was *no way out*.

"Now...let's play spin the bottle."

Did he really say that? To my horror, I actually heard the sound of an empty plastic bottle being twisted round on the fragmentary floor. "So doc, we play it like this...the one the bottle points at has to tell the *truth* about something."

"How can you see the bottle?"

"I can feel it, and it feels like its pointing at *you* as a matter of fact!"

"What...do you want to know?"

"I wanna know if you support freedom, doc. Good old American *freedom*."

"I , er..." Thinking frantically. "Yes...as long as it doesn't involve hate speech."

"That's right, doc. Hate speech is *not* free speech." (Parroting a now ancient and meaningless slogan.) "You support *true* free speech, then...which never includes hate speech?"

"Uh, yeah, sure."

"So...you don't mind speaking *freely* about why you think the way I use 'sand nigger' is an abstraction?"

Shit...he'd been reading my notebook. How had he done so? It must have been when he came to my room, and I'd turned to wash my face.

"The thing is, doc...I ain't never *said* the words 'sand nigger'. Never in my life. I don't use hate speech. I'm starting to think that *you're* the insane one, doc."

I cast about desperately for a way to change the subject. I suddenly realized that I didn't know where my gun was, and had little hope of finding it in the dark.

"Uh, isn't it my turn now to spin the bottle?"

"We're not playing that game any more, doc. We're playing the *faggot game*." Oh shit, he was going to try to rape me, I thought, groping about me for a weapon. My hand found a good-sized chunk of jagged concrete, and I clutched at it desperately.

"This is how the faggot game works, doc. You are *always* playing the game…and if you think about faggots, then you lose. And I'll blow your fucking brains out!"

"*What?* How on earth will you know if I'm thinking about…homosexuals?"

"You must've thought about them already, doc, because you mentioned them! Now, where's my rifle?"

"No!" I screeched, moving towards him with the chunk of concrete, fully intending to brain him.

"Haw haw haw…just a little joke, doc. All right, let's play another game…"

Another one of his stupid mind games followed, I don't remember which. The rest of that night is a terrible blur. Trapped underground with a madman, whose madness followed unpredictable patterns. And he never slept…

Yes, I know psychiatrists aren't supposed to use terms like 'madman', but it's okay because I'm no longer a registered psychiatrist. They stripped me of that privilege right after I grabbed a gun from the staff sergeant of the infantry squad who rescued us, and proceeded to shoot up the Combat Stress Control unit.

I write this report calmly but under armed guard, as the radio outside informs me that Buffo has just been awarded a Medal of Honor…not for his high number of kills, but rather for his aborted attempt on Scarface's life.

And I wait, and wait.

And all I can see is Buffo's empty visage in front of me, while bullets fly behind me out in camel lands.

So say goodnight to the West for me, please, and remember to turn out the lights.

7

## THE TESTIMONY OF
## MOHAMMED AL-ZAHABI
(via excerpts from his journal)

The lustre of the room was wonderful. This was the high point of my life, there could be no doubting it, and yet something was still lacking. I continued to play the dutiful poet, modest yet manly, while they went on congratulating me. My lesser part basked in it, just as my higher turned aside, with idle wryness, to contemplate the mystery of why the hole in my soul continues to wax larger.

But even my basking lesser part regarded them as philistine lunatics. For years, had I not turned out the most exquisite poems on love, philosophy and eternity, and with no recognition? Now, with one idle satirical verse about the creature called 'Buffo', I am suddenly admitted to the highest circles of war-ravaged Damascus, with old Colonel al-Ahmar proclaiming me a 'national treasure'.

It wasn't that my poem is a bad one – the taut construction of the verse, so different to my usual sinuous style, hints at new and previously unforeseen directions, new mimetic prisms for the Levantine Arabic dialect itself.

But it is no *achievement* – for with the subject being what he is, the satire virutally wrote itself. Syrians, to a man, believe Buffo to be a *faggot* (the Curia-aligned armies are riddled with such – maybe that's the only thing that keeps us fighting them). And while homosexualism doubtless happens here to a certain extent, too, it is not in the public square as with the broken, dying West, and many praise Allah for that.

In keeping with this theme, there was a point during the evening when someone turned on the TV to catch al-Akbar's latest war speech…for the great one has recently attained fluency in Arabic, and for some reason (good taste?) has chosen to learn the *Egyptian* dialect, and those present were curious to see how he handled it. (I confess the Egyptian dialect my own favourite, and intend to write poetry in it myself some day.)

But we didn't hear the results of al-Akbar's linguistic striving, because the Mossad were once again broadcasting gay porn into Syria, on all channels. Each time we counter their jamming technology they upgrade it, once more subjecting our populace to the visual sewer. If they seriously think they can destablise the Tate regime in this way they are gravely mistaken, as it merely turns the populace further against our 'esteemed' neighbour (whom no one doubts is behind the spectacle).

I took advantage of the loud expressions of disgust to leave the party early, playing the part of mysterious poet vanishing into the night. There was little chance of the military men taking my reticence as a sign of weakness, however, for they knew I had proved myself in war (in the splendid First Battle of Damascus) with the Dreamers and Poets Brigade, which, along with the International Brigade, has now been given official recognition by the Emir.

Having recovered from my war wound, the time was now right for me to volunteer for the new front: Cairo. (It was while waiting for my application to be considered that I wrote the idle poem on Buffo that has made me, overnight, into an unlikely celebrity.)

But a fire burns inside me. As poet, I have always had

to write in code (a code of words and symbols, of course...not a mere cipher like this journal), and all due to Islam – the religion of submission – from which I must hide my true feelings, my dreams across the waters.

For my allegiance is not to Allah but to the *neteru*, the great gods of Egypt, who existed before Ibrahim left Ur, and who exist still, giving lifeblood to my poetry. I give allegiance especially to the goddess Seshat, my true mistress, whose gift to me is that no woman shall ever have hold over me. Seshat, the goddess of history, who opens the doors of heaven...her spotted cloak the night sky, the stars, the leopardine world of poetry.

I remember well the trite tears of Rima, that beauteous wench I strung along these past six weeks in Damascus. I still hear her pitiful wailing, so fake-sounding to my poet's ear. I cast her off like so many dead skin cells, just as I have cast off so many others during my years as a soldier.

For in my sickly youth, with an artist's shyness and frail physique, I was scorned and rejected by these whores...and now am seen by the same empty vessels as 'desirable'! That is not due to my inner worth, though, but solely to my status in the Dreamers and Poets Brigade, much as I am now famous for a poem I consider a mere trifle, while my true work goes unnoticed and unappreciated.

So yes, I take delight in leading 'respectable' whores into thinking I like them, only to abandon them at their most vulnerable, when most deeply in love with me, for revenge is sweet, and I would not be a *man* if I didn't long for vengeance, pulsing and hot.

The price I pay for revenge, of course, is celebacy. Even masturbation is forbidden, because to do so I must conjure up the image of a woman in my mind's eye, and I will not give them even that pleasure. My semen is for the blood only, an offering for the goddess Seshat. That's how I write my poetry, the finest poetry in any Arabic dialect, and if the goddess leaves then my gift, too, will vanish.

But just lately, I have noticed a hole in my soul, which is growing undoubtedly larger. And for the first time since my youth, I am afraid of the future.

[…]

An even higher point of my life has come.

Al-Akbar himself saw fit to present me with an award for my little poem!

While no surprise that he would appreciate a work denigrating his would-be assassin, it is still a great honour that he would choose to confer the prize on me with his own hands, because he is *founder* of the Dreamers and Poets Brigade, and has done so much to restore the ideal of the Warrior Poet.

He presented me with a large copper medal engraved with semi-mythical figures from the past: T.E. Lawrence, Yukio Mishima and Henry Howard, Earl of Surrey. I received this medal with reverence and gratitude, studying al-Akbar's face as he presented me with it, but gleaning little from the shrapnel-scarred, careworn visage. This man is inscrutable, a mystery to myself and to others. Does he, like myself, have a Seshat in his soul, driving him to greater and higher deeds?

After the ceremony, I was privy to a game of chess between himself and the Emir. The latter lost, of course, and his facial expressions were far easier to read than those of his son-in-law. During the game these two giants casually discussed philosophy and architecture, and while they didn't say anything particulary profound, it was stimulating and inspiring to listen to.

Towards the end, they resumed negotiations which must have started earlier that day. It says much for al-Akbar's respect that I and several of my fellow Dreamers were allowed to be present without so much as a security pass. The key to these negotiations, it seemed, was the atomic bomb...for as a 'floating government', al-Akbar has so far found it impossible to get his hands on one, but believes he will lose prestige if he doesn't do so.

The Emir, on the other hand, is fervantly against this devil's weapon (a Jew's weapon, he calls it), but al-Akbar is worried that, if the Curia are defeated, the Samson Option will be pursued. There are also rumours an extreme Islamist sect may have attained the bomb, but no one knows anything concrete, making the world situation murkier and more amphibious.

Despite al-Akbar's lust for the bomb, he reminds me greatly of Neferirkare, that gentle Egyptian king of the fifth dynasty who forgave one of his ministers for an accidental transgression of sacred ritual. I wonder how someone like al-Akbar, clearly a Dreamer himself, has attained the level of power he has? He is a paradox, like the Bennu bird, the lord of jubilees, who is self-created and renews himself like the sun...like Atum, too, who made union with the feminine principle within himself, making love to his hand (or shadow) and creating divine children from loneliness.

And I, too, am lonely, even with the goddess within me...but my poems are my children. And although al-Akbar is rumoured to have an illegitimate child (the Emir's daughter having proven barren), I wonder if his *real* child is not the new world he is creating?

After the ceremony, I gave my medal and prize money (a bag of specially-minted gold coins) to a beggar in the street. There was an eerie sunset, and I am trepidatious as to what I will find in Cairo if allowed to proceed there.

[…]

I have been given the green light (along with four of my comrades) to travel to Cairo. I feel revitalised, like an ice age has ended. My limbs fill with relaxed energy as I plan what I shall do to those verminous fanatics currently raping the ruins of the sacred land of Kemet. This multicursal war has now truly become World War III, with only China and Russia refusing to pick sides. (Despite the Chinese making tentative overtures to al-Akbar, they are probably waiting cynically to see who is the victor. As for Russia, her motives are more mysterious.)

But I care not for such trifles – the excitement of the search is within me. And whatever I seek, I feel I will not find it in the squalid ferment of Cairo, but rather in the shifting desert sands. Time shall tell…

[…]

My blood has nearly boiled dry with the horrors I have encountered since arriving in Kemet (still glorious even in utter ruin). Cairo itself is vandalised by a vicious mob of Somalian mercenaries, and the worst of it is that they are ostensibly fighting for al-Akbar (not one of the great one's finest decisions). These 'allies' are agents of chaos, emissaries of Set. Far worse than the tomb robbers of old, they have literally *destroyed* ancient tombs and carvings in the suburbs of Cairo, as I saw with my own eyes on my first patrol – witnessing such an abominable act of desecration at a recent excavation near the temple of Ra-Atum at Heliopolis.

I turned to my brother Akram, a master weaver and Sufi, and my eyes filled with tears, before I hurled a grenade and blew at least five of the goblin-faced fiends limb from limb. Brother Akram shook his head sorrowfully, but did not take me to task for my act of fury, which anyone with a soul would have to admit was merciful, although not just – for justice would surely decree a slow and agonising death by torture for these wretched half-men.

A tourist plaque landed at my feet after the explosion, and I picked it up and wiped away the intestinal residue of one of the swart-skinned pirates, before perusing it. It spoke of the 'changeless valley of the Nile,' something I knew to be a gullible deception for tourists – for there are no changeless societies. It is true that Egypt changed more slowly than our own barbarous age, but it changed nonetheless. There is a world of difference in tone and form between the third dynasty (when the legendary Imhotep walked the earth) and the fourth, that of the mysterious Khufu and the pyramids of Giza. Likewise, between the fifth dynasty (the Sun Kings and their solar temples) and the sixth (when Osiris began his dominance) there is little comparison.

There are no static societies. What the Germans call 'Zeitgeist' is a very real phenomenon, and Seshat is its mistress. And while history rhymes, as they say, it never repeats.

Still, a successful society in my opinion is one that slows down the chaos as much as possible, and judged by that standard, Kemet was far greater than anything the present has to offer (although we may yet see what happens if al-Akbar wins the war).

Our modern attempts to kill change are pathetic, as exemplified by the Aswan High Dam, which so conveniently did away with the Nilus flood, and that was when Kemet truly died, for not even the coming of Christianity and Islam had such destructive power, *creating* Chaos in the name of destroying it.

[...]

Now I have been assigned guard duty at the Cairo Museum, which had already been trashed a generation eariler by the blasphemers of ISIS, doing the work of Set under the name of his bitterest enemy, the golden goddess. And now their successors continue the evil work, but thankfully under different names.

Before taking our places, we were given a short (too short!) tour of the ground floor of this incredible museum, and I saw for myself the hauntingly lifelike eyes of certain Old Kingdom statues, something no other culture has managed to replicate, ever. But unfortunately, the building has become a haven for Western tourists, who know the heavy guard here affords them protection from murderous pirates, and who walk past the most amazing relics with looks of smug and wooden blindness, their eyes deader by far than those of the statues. One of them actually snickered at me as he walked past.

"It's one of Scarlotti's men," he said to his companion. "What's a white supremacist doing *here?* Everyone knows Egypt was created by negros..." I laughed out loud at the fraud of this 'Black Egypt' theory, which he had fallen for even in spite of the statuary around him...and also at his description of me as a 'white supremacist'. For while I could probably pass for a southern European, I never thought of myself as anything other than a pagan Arab. The tourist, on the other hand, could easily have passed as a rotting corpse.

[…]

So it has begun again.

*Her* features, too, are fine like a European's, but her skin is copper. Not from the climate, though – it is the copper of love. The sign of ancient Kemet, the joy of living.

My first glimpse of her was a shoe, sticking out of a doorway. She was being raped by two Somalian savages, and they would doubtless have killed her afterwards had I not blown their miniscule brains out with my automatic.

I have hooked her in already, earning her devotion through sheer gratitude by saving her life. Naturally, I have been nothing but chivalrous in my actions since taking her under my wing (all her relatives in Cairo have been killed in the war – so much the better), and of course, when the time comes, I will joyfully abandon her.

She is a rare find, changing from Hathor to Sekhmet as she menstruates, but I believe I have the measure of her. All that is required, as usual, is self-control and patience. Just a little patience…

[…]

I took her for a camel ride in the Western Desert, outside of Kemet, in the Red Land, the scorpion land. We had armed guards for the journey – it is still possible for Dreamers and Poets to obtain such a privilege, al-Akbar having ordained that our kind are to be respected.

Things are very different out there in the land of Set, where the sky is that solid dome which gave birth to the monist heresy. A land of blood and brains and chaos, but also a place where heroes are engendered. The spirit of the heretic pharaoh Akhenaten (whom I believe to have been the son of a proto-Jewess) is said to haunt this desert eternally. His ghost would be the most terrible thing I could possibly come across, and even the thought of it makes me shudder intensely.

But her lithe and sinuous beauty took my mind away from these things (it is only fair to admit I had an erection for much of the journey.)

On returning to barracks in Cairo she hinted that she wanted me to enter the secure room in which she is ensconced, and while I managed to smile and refuse, my body gave greater resistance than I am accustomed to.

This one, I fear, is not going to be easy.

[...]

My beliefs have been made public – not something I intended. During a patrol, we came across one of the New Gnostics, a heresy that grows rapidly in the chaos of wartorn Egypt (I believe they have little in common with the gnostics of antiquity.) This cretin was preaching his vile belief, worse than Islam in my mind, that there is nothing but an *elemental malice* behind the universe, and that all that we hold good and beautiful will ultimately prove illusion, being created in the first place merely as a method of torment (once we have grasped the truth) by this same elemental malice.

How does one refute such a repugnant heresy as this? I am afraid that I did so with an uncharacteristic lack of subtlely (what is wrong with me of late, that I can no longer keep my emotions in check?), yelling at the repulsive preacher and calling him a cheap and pox-ridden charlatan who was no gnostic, for he knew not truth.

"And what *is* truth?" he asked me with a caustic sneer. I started shrieking at him about the gods, the *neteru*, the true and noble standard-bearers of the cosmos. And none truer than Maat, goddess of cosmic order, who defends against Isfet, chaos, injustice…Isfet, the invisible thief who sneaks through windows at night filling our subconscious mind with lazy thoughts, with egalitiarian and nihilist thoughts. Isfet, the true master of this 'gnostic' preacher, who I now surged forward to punch, while my comrades were forced to restrain me. I can still see his crooked sneer, and I punch the air in front of me.

"Order can't exist *without* chaos," he cackled. "And therefore both are illusion."

"No!" I yelled. "One can't exist without the other, yes, that's why Set originally helped the gods…but they're *not* equal. Maat must be *fought for*. That was the king's role, the pharaoh's role…to destroy Isfet, even if it can't ultimately be destroyed…and that is why he was crowned king."

"There are no kings anymore, imbecile…not even your precious Scarlotti."

"It is the poet who must now fight for Maat, you vermin…and *this* is high religion, not the puerile need for salvation or extinction."

He was leaving, doubtless afraid he would lose face with his followers if I continued to better him in debate. But I was greatly concerned that his disabling heresies might spread among the young in Cairo and elsewhere, and if my brothers had not fervently restrained me, I would have put a bullet in him, just as I had with the last agents of Isfet I had come across (the Somalian rapists).

But now I had another problem to deal with. My comrades, who were shaking with emotion at this confrontation (which the more orthodox among them would necessarily have regarded as a confrontation between two opposing heresies), now saw me for what I undoubtedly am – an unabashed polytheist. That is a dangerous thing to be in the Arabic world, even in liberal Egypt, and tongues will wag; there is no stopping it. Now I am to be held suspect by Muslims *and* Neo-Gnostics. That is a pleasure to me, but I must watch my back.

I take comfort in the fact that the *Emir* is now also considered suspect by many for his refusal to seek the Bomb...although I almost wish that he would, for I am loyal to both him and al-Akbar, and have no wish to see them fall out again.

[...]

Already the gossip has spread.

*She* confronted me about it today, claiming concern for my welfare. My own poet 'comrades' have been casting strange looks at me, and it already feels that I am no longer part of their brotherhood – but if that is so, then *I* am the true poet and not they.

I half expected her, too, to abandon me...but if anything the opposite has occurred. Not only does she say she will stick with me regardless, but has even dropped hints (subtle yet undeniably there) that she may sympathise. Inwardly I groaned, for if true, this will make it harder still to break with her when the time comes, as it must come. And yet abandon her I will, fulfilling justice – Maat.

I spent the night in her arms, but chastely. Even this is a violation of my usual methods, and also very difficult, as she constantly arched herself against me in certain places...not insistently, but enough to make me burn inside.

Corrosion, corrosion, all is corrosion.

Only by resisting it do I create order.
*Maat.*

[…]

Now al-Akbar has announced that he has attained the bomb, via one of his renegade genius scientists, and peacefully!

Is he bluffing? This man is a chess player, thinking many moves ahead, and not everything he says can be taken as a straightforward statement of fact. For all that, it is quiet tonight in Cairo…I have an unusual feeling that people are *thinking*.

If he *does* have the bomb, what does it mean?

I imagine it as a malevolent sun: Ra's Boat of Millions of Years, only with Set at the helm.

But there is a famous story about the pharaoh Menkaure, who turned six years into twelve by keeping lamps burning at night, thus delaying the death which fate had ordained for him. Perhaps that is what al-Akbar's announcement means – that he is playing for time. Cannon, too, were regarded as demonic five centuries ago, and so perhaps I am merely out of tune with the Zeitgeist?

As for *her*, my resistance crumbled further, so I have removed her from the barracks, setting her up with her own secure house, pulling a few strings in order to do so. I imagine her dancing naked there, alone, and my loins are inflamed. Surely this torment will soon be over?

[…]

Disaster has struck.

*The Emir has fallen to the assassin's bullet.*

Now I am racked with guilt for being in Egypt, and not in Syria where perhaps I could have helped to prevent it...but no, it is impossible to say *what* I could have done. All I can see in front of me is the slow motion footage from Al Jazeera, showing the Emir's brains exiting his skull in a high-pressure spurt. The projectile, sent by Set, did its job all too well, and the blond beast has fallen. So who will pick up his torch? And what awaits *me?*

I fear the Middle East will be plunged into heavier and heavier chaos, making the current war seem but a trifle in comparison. Isfet, and its emissary Set, are now in the ascendent.

[...]

Sure enough, many of the Emir's men have refused to flock to the banner of al-Akbar's Multicursal Curia (not actually a Curia, of course, but an Imperium...the name is surely a parody), and presumably because their blood has been poisoned by the religion of submission. Now some are flocking to new 'emirs' (pretenders), and others are repudiating them with loud words and many.

All I can do is watch the sun set, and the slow and inexorable rise of Set over Kemet.

Tonight, I am sure, I will dream that I am dancing with a scorpion.

I must go to her.

[...]

116

I jogged slowly along the bloodstained roads of Cairo, unsure as to what I would find. Brutal machine gun fire dotted the running poetry of my journey through ancient starlight. Every apartment block was a cavern, every house a den of monsters. I saw sights, but they flashed by like apparitions, so I couldn't be sure if they had ever existed.

I saw a man standing *over* his own assassin, one bloody hand holding in his entrails as he made a calm formal gesture with the other, while his murderer laughed and reclined in the alley, gun forgotten next to him, as both basked in their roles in an affable cosmic comedy. It seemed that the murdered one would surely spell some humorous word in his own blood, before finally expiring, but I would never know what it was.

Then, further north, I saw a mob (of the kind I detest) clamouring for a leader. They were literally *demanding* that someone lead them, but no one stepped forward for the task. I might have contemplated it myself, but they stank of offal and corruption, so I hurried forward into segmented night, another link flashing in the chain up ahead.

Next I remember, I was actually in *her* neighbourhood, slowing down to a brisk walk, before locating her building with pounding heart.

*She was there.*

We embraced, ecstatic, and I held her tightly as the sound of gunfire drew gradually closer. Her guards had deserted her. A horse ran past the entryway rolling flame-reflecting eyes…and for the first time, we kissed, our tongues becoming quicksilver, merging in the smoke-stale air, directed by our whims and by the unpredictable rhythms of the gunfire.

But even in my bliss, I realised I had to get her out of there, and that the neighbourhood around the house was now a danger zone. Swiftly we began the reverse journey, along quieter backstreets to avoid the hotspots of violence. My arm was around her waist, which was shimmering as she moved, the last emissary of beauty in this benighted city.

Sights were different in the alleyways, running roughly concurrent with the dangerous routes I had taken on the way out. On a crumbling balcony overhanging the street we were greeted by the sight, unearthly, of an ancient crone watering potted plants from an antique jug whose intricate design made me think of that twisting tongue that had just entwined with my own, and would soon do so again.

I hurried her along, panting, until we were once more in the shadow of the barracks. The guards recognised her, and looked resentful. All their effort spent guarding a womanising heretic (and his whore), while Cairo is on fire! I sympathised, but not too much.

The barracks were deserted apart from the guards, and I surmised that my brother poets were off fighting chaos in the vast urban jungle. This time I was determined to know her carnally, even though it broke every rule of my existence.

I tore the garments from her shoulders and led her into the chamber she had formerly inhabited. Then I lay her down on the bed, pouring oil across her breasts, and rubbing it into her soft copper skin while she stared at me with round eyes, calmly realising that she was being prepared for intercourse. She would neither resist nor enthuse, the gaze said...she was in my hands, and pliable. Her only concern would be keeping my affections *after* the act...and for this reason things might still work, although I had violated my own rules.

I knew her then...and the noise she made was enough to shake the buildings, as was the noise *I* made when I ejaculated – like a rushing geyser of bellowing steam, pent up beneath the earth for a thousand years. My penis, unused to issuing semen in this way, felt scorched, as though something caustic has just passed through it, and I groaned in agony as she rocked gently in my trembling arms.

In the end, she went to sleep on my shoulder, and with some difficulty I prised her away, stepping out the front door to breathe the night air.

The guards had abandoned us, and I could hardly blame them…fancy having to listen to the roaring of rutting elephants while their own families were in danger elsewhere in the city!

But now the thousand and first night had arrived…

I reentered, and she awoke, smiling sleepily at me from behind a soft veil of bliss – which I demurred not from penetrating, ejaculating misery inside her roseate joy.

"I'm going, now," I growled. "And *you* will stay here, worthless cunt."

"What? I am confused…*don't you love me?*" And she burst into tears, exactly as the others had done before her. All so predictable.

But there was something different this time, something about the rote, dulled feeling of my own words as I heaped insults on her. And something, too, about the fury with which she sprang at me, clawing at my eyes at the very moment she screeched that she loved me. I was weeping as I knocked her unconscious, abandoning the barracks, and Cairo, never to return.

Yes…this time something was different.

From whence comes the sudden feeling that the hole in my soul can be *no longer sewn up?*

[…]

Somehow, amidst the chaos, I managed to board a military flight to Damascus...the plane climbs the air even as I write. It is doubtful I shall ever return to Kemet, of which I now realise something *has* survived, in spite of the Persians, the Romans, the Arabs, the Turks, Napoleon, the Curia and the rest of them. For something is still out there, at the edge of the two lands, red and black.

A soldier on the plane dances a crazed Western-style dance (I think it is called a 'pogo'), while his comrades laugh and cheer him on.

I go dizzy at the edges. Can't write any more.

[...]

Last night, my first back in Damascus, I had a remarkable dream. I dreamt that an Islamic extremist faction had nuked the Great Pyramid. In this dream, the pyramid (which has never been proved to be a tomb, incidentally; some believe it to have been an initation chamber) looked exactly as it must have done during the reign of Khufu, with its limestone casing and capstone...the Benben, perch of the mighty Bennu bird. In short, it looked like a futuristic temple.

And when the nuclear device went off, a *secret chamber* was revealed in the rubble. I woke before I could see what was in it – but I knew it was something immensely important.

I am clutching at it now, wondering what it was...

[...]

I turn the news off and *my dream is true*. It was a premonition, and I am devastated, shaking. The Islamists have actually destroyed that which could never be destroyed. What good is al-Akbar's bomb (even if he wasn't bluffing about it)? He can't bomb them back. The nature of warfare has changed.

But, oh, of all things I have dreamt that might have turned out true, *a secret chamber has been revealed beneath the rubble!* The elderly Zahi Hawass led the inspection party, tottering out on his walking stick in his radiation-proof suit. But there was nothing inside the chamber – nothing.

Hawass wept, and so did I. My resistance to *her* was Isfet, not Maat, for Maat is like riding a wave, or music, and only now do I see this. It is difficult, the way of Maat, even for poets, even for kings…

All I can do now is to go back to Cairo and search for her in the radioactive ruins.

My gnosis…knowing I will never actually find her.

## 8

## THE TESTIMONY OF
## ADAM BRAY

"Ryebread! How are things?"

Those were the words that first indicated I was becoming too attached to the senator, that I was doing my job too well, and that it was probably time to move on. I was looking out for *his* interests at the expense of my own, and that would never do.

'Ryebread', it appeared, was the nickname of one Jed Turner, the senator's liason with various DC subcommittees. It should have been the first time I had ever heard the nickname, but it wasn't…and for that reason, in spite of the risks entailed, I thought I should probably bring certain matters to the senator's attention. Thus I left the restaurant in a downpour of rain, unnoticed by Turner or his aquaintance.

It wasn't only they I had to fear, however, for the sensitive nature of the information meant the senator himself might very well show me the door, leaving me unemployed, which was not a good thing to be in the Beltway at that time.

The information was as follows:

Weeks earlier I had found a small piece of notepaper in the stairwell to the underground carpark beneath the building housing the senator's office. On it was a scrawled memo which effectively said this: that Senator Edwin Blogue was a confirmed moron, who had been appointed to the senate for similar reasons to Caligula's horse – namely, to show any dissidents that *they* (meaning the Curia) could appoint whosoever they wanted in Presidential America. And to make it doubly clear, Blogue was actually being considered for a position in President Hodge's new cabinet (now that the laws had been changed to allow the president a third term in office).

But here was the interesting thing: the note was addressed to one 'Ryebread', who had apparently dropped it by mistake on his way down to the carpark. The droll name initially made me believe it to be some kind of practical joke, until I heard Turner addressed so in the restaurant, proving beyond doubt the earnest nature of the note's contents.

I knocked at the senator's door, awaiting the phlegmatic voice to bid me enter. After strangling a brief burst of fear, I gritted my teeth and showed him the note (which I had put in my wallet and forgotten about until this afternoon). He perused it until his jowls wobbled, and for a moment I thought he was going to react with anger…but to my surprise his face assumed a blank look, and he handed it back to me.

"I believe I know who the addressee of the note is, sir…the 'Ryebread' referred to is actually…"

But he held up his hand in a gesture of dismissal.

"These things aren't important," he said impassively. "But, now that you're here, Bray, please tell me what you think of this new dietery plan..." He handed me a printout with the details of some new fad diet, to which I gave a noncomittal "Looks okay", and that seemed to satisfy him. It was a matter of common knowledge that Blogue's struggle with his weight was more important to him than the plight of his people…even so, it was a lacklustre struggle, one he probably knew he would never win.

Next day we were summoned to a meeting of the

Senate Subcommittee for Stamping Out Hate, where an important member of the Curia (I forget his name) gave a rundown on events surrounding the Antichrist's alleged obtainment of the Bomb (the recent *actually occurring* nuclear blast at Giza being scarcely mentioned).

After his speech, the assembled senators began to robotically denounce the Antichrist, and none more so than Edwin Blogue, whose protestations sounded so melodramatically fake that even some of the other senators looked at him in fear, as if he might be a Curia spy.

This led them in turn to heighten their *own* denunciations, which caused Blogue to likewise grunt louder, and so forth, in a kind of gathering feedback loop, whose echoed squeals grew so thunderous at one point that the floor began to shake.

I admit there was a moment, just a moment, when I wondered if perhaps Blogue *was* playing some convoluted role as Curia spy, but dismissed it as impossible…unless one meant he was playing the Curia's role neatly by virtue of sheer stupidity. I shook my head, wondering why I even cared about the fate of such a man, who was sure to come to a sticky end sooner or later (for health reasons if nothing else).

Later that day, I remember being present in the senator's office when he was briefed on the Antichrist's work to fulfill his Palestine plan, which was now being thwarted, not just by Israel itself, but also by forces within the Islamic world. The entire Middle East seemed dark on him now, for varying reasons, and the Curia were endeavoring to take full advantage of this. I took in more of all this than the senator, of course, who (as was his wont) nodded off at one point.

After that, we attended the Church of the Multicultural Christ in DC for an evening Holiday Service, as it was December 24th. The reverend had a disapproving look on his face throughout the service, I know not why…perhaps the overwhelming whiteness of the attendees disappointed him. But afterwards he took the senator aside, to ask him how the 'heretic generals' like Frampton (now in prison) would be treated. The Senator held up a puffed flipper to cut him short.

"Please don't ask me for leniency, reverend. Even a man of God cannot sway us."

"Leniency?" snarled the reverend, in disbelief. "I was going to ask you to fry them alive!"

This cute theological discussion was interrupted, however, by a siren-burst outside, followed by angry shouts, and the remaining congregation piled out to investigate.

To the reverend's utter horror, someone had spraypainted the church building, changing its sign to 'Church of the *Multicursal* Christ'. The police had apprehended the perpetrator, having caught him in the act during a routine patrol, but imagine our surprise when we observed the villain was a coal-black negro! This seemed to cause the senator's brain to short-circuit somewhat, and he announced he was making his way home for a festive glass of bourbon and cola…then he actually invited me back to his house, which I had never visited before. I thought it would be impolitic to refuse. Drinking commenced as soon as we entered his limo.

"I hope they horsewhip that bastard," he muttered as we drove off.

"Major-General Frampton?"

"No…the blackamore, I mean."

Sigh. Slow and fat…behind the times in acceptable language. That was our senator.

After a moment of silence he slurped his drink.

"Desecrating the Multicultural Christ is unforgivable," he gurgled, and belched. I had the feeling I was sitting in the car with a distended corpse.

Yes…perhaps it was time to move on.

We were driving through downtown DC now, and an old bum rumaged briskly in a bin, searching out his holiday meal. As we passed, he turned to stare, and I swear he could see through the one-way glass of the limo…it seemed like he was looking right at me. He was clutching something he had pulled out of the bin – it looked like a half-full bottle of white wine. I envied his find, which seemed better than the bourbon and cola I was about to drink for career reasons. The wino didn't have a job to worry about, and he looked bright-eyed and bushy-tailed. Still, all in all, I didn't think I would take to the bum's life, mainly because I couldn't stand the cold. Central heating is an indispensable element of my life.

It was certainly warm in the limo, and I began to nod off, drifting into one of those little punctuated half-waking dreams that send electric shocks through the gaps in your ribcage. In this dream, the senator and I were floating through Venice in a gondola, which he was slowly sinking with his weight. I tried to steady him, but couldn't get a grip on his fat rolls, despite the rough outfit he was wearing (made of old potato sacks, I think).

Then it happened – the senator fell, with an abyssal splosh, into the cold-dark water, flipping over the gondola…and I was suddenly catapulted onto the top of St. Mark's Campanile, where I could see, with infrared clarity, the entire city of Venice sinking rapidly into the swamp…little earthen mounds with fires burning atop them, all that was left of the Most Serene Republic.

But out in the distance was a bigger beacon…I strained my eyes, but couldn't make out who had lit it, or even guess why.

Then I snapped to, suddenly remembering where I was. The senator was still muttering about the church vandalism as we pulled up outside the Georgetown townhouse where he lived when in DC, somewhat smaller than his Tennessee mansion. His wife (childless and fatter than he) welcomed us in personally, explaining that she had given the maid the evening off, and that the leave had been of the paid variety. She led us through corridors of an old, elegant house (cheaply and tackily decorated), into a sitting room, where my eye was unavoidably drawn to a signed photo of Johnny 'Buffo' Stokes on the far wall. The senator poured, and we sat morosely sipping our bourbon (and a mint julep for the lady). No one spoke. So much for the festive season.

A second drink livened things briefly by causing the senator to belch loudly, making his wife titter nervously, before silence descended again. But this was shattered minutes later by a frantic hammering at the door. The excited-looking guest turned out to be none other than the usually-sedate Jed 'Ryebread' Turner.

I glanced at him curiously – for now that I knew his secret I half expected his face to look different, but it didn't. It looked embarassingly mundane, like that of a teacher of dances which had gone out of fashion ten years ago…the workaday Beltway soft-face.

"I was in the neighbourhood when I heard the news myself, and I thought I'd drop by in person to give you a run-down on the *incredible events*…and to wish you a season's greetings, of course."

Blogue sounded distant as he casually asked what the news was. Time to seemed to gather round his ponderous mass like light round a black hole, his coastal edges doing their best to freeze it, and even Turner's professional voice seemed hollow in Blogue's shadow.

"Well, firstly, senator, a sizeable faction of Scarlotti's own troops in the Middle East have betrayed him…completely deserted him, in fact."

"The Antichrist, deserted!" Blogue looked surprised for the first time.

"And not only that, he's been abandoned by his

largest unit of Somalian mercenaries. They were lured by the promise of better pay from the Curia."

"That's wonderful!"

"We…I mean *they*…have been working on it for some time. But it's not all good news, senator. Momentous, but not good."

"Well, spit it out, man."

"Scarlotti has fled to the so-called North West Republic."

"*What?!*"

"That's right. He's on our very shores."

The senator sat bolt upright, looking like a rat had just scurried up his ass. I never saw him move so quick.

Next day, December 25, we attended an emergency Senate briefing session, and the feral hordes were out in full force, kept in check only by police guns. And I mean *guns*, not water cannon, as some of these communist and anarchist types were actually equipped with armored vehicles, like something out of an old film called *The Road Warrior*. Aside from a group with signs stating their opposition to 'government microchipping' (who seemed to be shunned by other protesters), I had no idea what the mob was actually against. Were they there to take the side of the Antichrist (which would put them on the side of racism and fascism) or were they frantically urging the government to go to war against him, launching a full scale invasion of the Pacific Northwest (which would put them in the camp of conservative Christian Zionists)? Either way, the stench of their body odor was unbearable. I could smell it through the car's air vents, and it almost made me retch.

The fact that a Mossad agent was due to address the assembled senators may have had some bearing on things – for while Israel was still popular with the Hodge regime (and the aforementioned Christian Zionists), the far left had been moving towards a more consistently egalitarian position for ages, and now rabidly hated Israel. This was in keeping with the international strategy of the Curia in general (interestingly, because there were a lot of Jews in it), and fewer people now listened to the Right's argument that Jews are *entitled* to hypocrisy on immigration issues because they are somehow 'different' or 'special'. Also, fewer Jews themselves now identified with Israel, and fewer secular Israelis felt inclined to give military service for the benefit of what they increasingly saw as a parasitical ultra-Orthodox class. So will the Curia soon make 'Open Borders for Israel' an actual policy? In other words, will the Zionist part of the Curia's project be *abandoned?* Heavy thoughts…

I then realized it probably *was* the Mossad agent they were protesting against, because they were hurling most of their abuse against a group of Evangelicals of the kind who literally worship Jews, and who were hoping to get a glimpse of their hero (the special agent) as his car left the underground tunnel.

It turned out that the agent, David Peretz, was the first speaker, and he briefed us on new evidence from a Syrian double operative which shed valuable light on the Antichrist's bizarre belief system. Apparently, he subscribed to something called 'esoteric ethnopluralism', which Peretz proceeded to elucidate for us. Most of the senators looked baffled at his description of this strange creed, which was utterly beyond their ken – and mine, I admit (Blogue had already fallen asleep). Senator O'Neill, who had recently been at the centre of the Four Seasons scandal, until it emerged that the prostitutes involved were transexual (and was now regarded as a hero of the conservative movement as a result), probably gave voice to the thoughts of many when he said: "this Morning Star business is surely a sign of devil worship." Those assembled snorted like pigs, reminding me of ancient tales my mother had told me about Senate hearings into 'backwards masking' on old heavy metal records.

Agent Peretz looked down from the podium, smiling at the contented self-righteous boars and sows he had just thrown some scraps to.

"Gentlemen and ladies," he shouted. "We have nothing to worry about. The whole *civilized* world is against Scarlotti. He will fall!"

Thunderous applause followed...Hodge's people especially lapped it up (and even Blogue woke and began flopping his flippers together), for they always revelled in the straight-talking of visiting Israeli speakers, especially on matters where they wouldn't tolerate straight-talking in their *own* ranks.

But their optimism was badly misplaced.

Over the next few weeks, the news filtering out of the northwest went from worse to *far* worse. Border tensions in that area had never really died down since the uprising, but now that the Antichrist had taken command, Hodge himself had given the green light for an invasion.

He reckoned without the military, however. Now the Antichrist's reforms had been overturned, the forces consisted mainly of fat junkies, mincing transexuals and slovenly gangbangers. As a result, at the Battle of Missoula, the Antichrist actually managed to extend the Republic's borders well into Montana.

Soon after that, he captured several urban areas that had formerly been outside the Republic: Seattle, Olympia, Eugene and Portland. These liberal, pro-Presidential cities must have boiled with rage at such a fate. One celebrity (you remember her, no doubt) was caught trying to paddle a kayak down the coast to California, and was placed on a work detail in Aberdeen as punishment. (After that, no one else tried to flee.)

I remember walking through downtown DC in a daze, trying to digest the fact that there was now a truly separate country on American soil (for until its new leader's arrival, the Republic had always seemed a transient affair to me, and I had expected it to collapse in the next breeze). And everywhere I walked, people seemed to be running round like headless chickens. The crazies were everywhere, or perhaps the new order had *sent* them crazy. One strange beanlike creature was screaming: "I am compelled by law to resist all laws" or something similar, and an aged harridan berated everyone she could on the dangers of "relaxing one's vigilence." The Trots were out in force, too, screeching against Hodge, Nor'westers, and even the Curia itself (which they now apparently mistrusted), but they were just one element in a broken mix. You could feel America's dying breath round every corner you turned.

What was happening in the North West itself, however, was unknown at that point. There was much talk about how incongruous it seemed, a cosmopolitan Nietzschean aristocrat being made president (apparently by popular mandate) of a democratic republic run by hardcore Nazi monoculturalists. My parents' generation, tuned in to Rush Limbaugh, could never have foreseen it. But the seasons they change, and time has a funny way of tilling the soil. My dream of the gondola blazed vividly back to me.

All speculation about whether our particular Antichrist was a 'white nationalist' (he had never claimed to be anything of the kind) was soon answered, however, by the interception of a presidential broadcast, wherein the Antichrist now gave an *actual commitment* to the ideals of white nationalism, placing himself about as far out on the Curia's whackjob-scale as it was possible to go. The Curia gleefully disseminated the broadcast to all the world, hoping to drum up further hatred against their adversary.

But a funny thing happened – now that the Antichrist

had declared himself an actual white nationalist, over thirty *non-white* countries rushed to pledge allegiance to him, abandoning the Curia! Apparently he was now seen as having more integrity by virtue of openly working for his own people. To put it mildly, this was something the Curia had failed to predict...

One power which came over to his side was old uncle Chow (smiling China). This wasn't good...but I couldn't drum up feeling enough to care. And when negotiations with the Curia recommenced, the latter were forced to acknowledge him as Imperator over half the world, with Russia as the only neutral power (the papers, you remember, were signed in Moscow).

More people were rushing about like headless chickens, and frankly this period is a bit of a blur to me. I do remember the stupified look the senator wore for several weeks afterwards, however.

I also remember our final meeting.

By that time, the senator had reconciled himself to the situation, and (mistakenly regarding himself as something of an expert on Antichrist) believed he would be one of those chosen to negotiate further on behalf of America. For days he had been sitting there, waiting for a call that would never come.

But peace was here! Finally, world peace; though few in the Beltway seemed happy about it. I thought the time propitious, however, so I did it...I asked the senator for a raise.

"At a time like this, Bray?" he spluttered. "What on earth are you *thinking?*"

I left then, with a song in my heart. Multicultural, Multicursal, Christ, Antichrist...let us bide a whiles, part a while...

*For a fair maid of England hath told me*
*That the crows are departed the Tower.*

*So I'll seek for my bailiwick elsewhere,*
*Sniffing out some new dungheap of power.*

9

## THE TESTIMONY OF
## EDMUND T. SPITZLER
(via excerpts from his journal)

Dear diary, please excuse my long silence. Dinner with Leonard; discussed new delays in wardrobe, amongst others. Wine from Walla Walla, best available at present, not exactly Hippocrene, and then he showed me the new design for Kundry's Act II dress, which finally looks about right, walking a middle line between underseductive and slutty. I only hope it will be ready for opening night, the only truly important night for all that others may say. Our chief problems lie with the orchestra now (why couldn't it have been Purcell, not Wagner?). Will require general meeting on that, not two crusties roseate with mediocre vino.

Taxi home a nightmare, driver utter Neanderthal. Yes, I know we're not supposed to use that word disparagingly (have read regime booklet showing Neanderthals ancient master race whose blood flows diluted in our veins, Cascadian fruit juice to their exquisite claret), but I don't care. This man looked like what Neanderthal *used* to mean, there's no other way of putting it. Craggen monobrow, sullen insolence…itched to beat him with my stick, but checked self in time. *Remember probation conditions.* Almost regret the day I was given this beautiful ornate walking stick by Marie Lefévre, descendent of Victor Hugo. Feels like it was made for cracking philistine skulls, and harder to resist doing so than with lesser canes (also, wouldn't have minded giving Hugo a good crack with it).

Returned to my den of splendor to unexpectedly find wayward wife there. Not just *there*, but rubbing herself against me like a cat. How fortunate that I am allergic to felines of all descriptions. Grilled her with suspicious annoyance on why she was acting 'sexy' and 'seductive'. She was forced to confess: had *very* bad news, and wanted to break it gently. I jokingly quoted Hemingway: "What, did you fuck a nigger?"

"*Worse*, from your point of view," she said with a different kind of cattiness, arching finely-combed eyebrows.

"Yes?"

"Two bits of bad news, actually. First, the costumes from Portland were finally delivered…but they went to the wrong theatre."

"You mean…"

"*Whizz* got hold of them by mistake."

"So…that explains the delay. Well, he knows what the Flowermaidens will be wearing. It's not the end of the world."

"No. It's worse than that."

"How?"

"He didn't send them on like he should have…he just threw them in a dumpster out the back of the theatre, and they went to landfill before he could recover them."

"*What?!*"

"Says he didn't realize whose they were…saw them in his office where the delivery men had put them, and thought they were just cheap tat someone had left to be thrown out. Only realized his mistake when he saw the invoice on his desk a few days later."

I stumped around the room, speechless with rage, swishing my stick left and right, and almost thrashing the wife in my blind fury.

"Hey, watch it!"

"He's lying, that philistine…of *course* he fucking realized."

"You don't know…"

"I *do* know. It wasn't just a calculated insult…it was an attempt at sabotaging our entire production."

"Calm down, Edmund, I implore you."

"The truce is over, the rift is reopened. I want revenge…revenge!"

"Now don't go round there. You know your probation conditions."

"*Fuck* my probation conditions. Anyway, there are other ways of taking revenge."

"You should calm down, anyhow, because I told you the lesser news first. The second thing is…*our daughter is pregnant.*" She blurted it quickly, and my anger immediately changed to a feeling of creeping uneasiness. Karl, Stella's steady boyfriend and presumably the father, has gone off on a secret mission of some sort into Presidential territory, apparently with the blessing of Il Maestro himself, and hasn't been seen for two months. Quite possibly dead and, as the relationship hasn't been legitimized by marriage, won't qualify her for widowhood, merely single mother status, which isn't looked on favourably by the regime. Can only hope Il Maestro himself will take pity on her and change her official status somehow…not that she'd care, never has. A rebel, like Wagner…I don't understand rebels. Give me Purcell any day.

"So," I muttered. "I'll be a grandpa."

"You should visit her tomorrow. She's upset. She still doesn't know if Karl is alive or dead."

"Yes, I'll visit."

"You really, really should."

"Yes, I will. In the morning."

"Yes." And then she kissed me, that wife of mine. Led

her to the bedchamber for the first time in months. I spare you the details, dear diary, but at 2am feel less desire to swing my ornate stick than I have in…well, months.

[…]

I arrived at the crumbling old wooden house that Stella calls home, expecting to be attacked by bats, ravens or wolves. The darkness seemed to grow as I walked down the path, swinging my stick, and I fancied I could hear the rustle of little people in the bushes. Then Stella opened the door, and all was light. There seemed to be a halo around her visage, tinged with sadness as it was. I dropped the joke forming on my lips about her gothic abode, opting to hug her instead. She seemed more reserved than usual.

We sat in two ricketty chairs in the kitchen, waiting for some kind of herbal tea to steep.

"No wine then?"

She shook her head. "Mom told you?"

"Yes. And Karl's the father?"

"Yeah."

"And no news?"

"Nope."

I rolled off some cliched words of consolation. She took them silently, then a spark came back into her eyes.

"It's embarassing you're looking out for *me*, dad. I'm a Wolf, supposed to be alienated from boomers and all that." I was going to point out that I was born in '81, and by no means a boomer, but checked myself when I remembered that 'boomer' has now become a generic term for anyone over forty. *Everyone* will be a boomer some day, unless they have the good grace to die young.

Plus, I sensed a certain self-mocking deceit in her tone, although it was hard to be sure…I've never been sure of anything regarding my daughter, to be honest. She's a strange creature, like all Wolves.

I glanced round the kitchen, but it conveyed little of her lifestyle and beliefs. It might have been that of a psychedelic carpenter, or paramilitary gardening guru. In fact, it was the kitchen of a Wolf of Joy.

"And do you regard the new regime as less hypocritical and corrupt than the old one, my darling daughter?"

"Yes."

"Then why haven't the Wolves disbanded?"

"There's no membership list, so nothing to disband. You're a Wolf by your deeds, and those alone."

"Ah…that's right. *Deeds and death*, your watchword. From Wagner, I believe." Many of the Wolves had nearly abandoned their mission the year before the war, the same year Stella became one of them. That was the year the globalist upper-middle classes began having 'Wolves of Joy' theme-parties, where they would celebrate their own hypocrisy by reenacting pranks from a book called *The Hungry Wolves of Van Diemen's Land*.

"So why didn't you abandon your mission?"

"We realized that if we care what small people think then we're no bigger ourselves, of course."

"But what's your *point* these days? In the North West of all places, which is officially anti-globalist?"

"We must be vigilant."

"Doesn't that bore you?"

"No."

"You need a project…an opera or something."

"Yes…we have a current project, actually. Our new aim is to go to war *for* the Archetype."

"How do you do that?"

"We're still figuring it out."

I left it at that. As we sipped the disgusting tea, we discussed her pregnancy, especially in light of the fact that the new regime is staunchly anti-feminist and frowns upon single mothers. (Il Maestro has respected this, and other North Western tenures, since his coronation as king, despite what his personal proclivities might be). In point of fact, the regime's attitude to women is very much like that of the Nazis' 'Kinder, Küche Kirche', except with the Kirche scratched out to avoid offending the regime's pagans (whom Il Maestro favours over the Christians, though he does everything in his power to avoid religious discord).

Did Stella have a problem with this?

"No."

No. No matter how 'restricted' women are, she will always do what she wants. Our conversation petered out, and I told her I would return shortly, in spite of my busy schedule, to bring her some wine, so she need never drink that putrid tea again.

"I'm pregnant, dad. No alcohol." She smiled for the first time.

"Oh yes. Well, I'll see you soon I expect."

We hugged once more, and I left. Perhaps this crisis will enable us to form a friendship of sorts at long last. Every cloud has a silver lining. But I note that neither of us expressed any joy in the imminent arrival of a new life in the world. Are we subconsciously afraid? World peace is here, so we've all been told…does peace make us paranoid? Or is there something around the corner, some dreadful, unimagined horror? I wandered the streets of Seattle, pondering these matters, and, even though crime is now virtually zero, I felt glad to have my stick at hand. I seemed to feel a storm coming, though one seldom knows how far off such things are. It isn't *like* me to feel such things…I hope the vile tea hasn't given me some sort of clairvoyance.

To deflect these thoughts I considered the good and bad points of the new regime. Although hardly on its side (or anyone else's) the fact that my lack of strong disapproval in itself seems to cause many so-called friends to disapprove of *me* makes me mildly sympathetic to the regime out of sheer spite. And then there is our sovereign (can it be true?) Il Maestro, who seems like a character from an opera himself...Wagner rather than Purcell, admittedly. (And, how many of the luvvie 'disapprovers' have refused work offered to them by the regime out of principle? None! Hypocrites...)

I do like the dramatic flair with which His Majesty, Il Maestro, has appointed government officials with such ancient, evocative titles: seneschals, justiciars, dapifers, logothetes and so forth. So the Republic and the Free Cities have now become a Kingdom, which itself exists within an Imperium that covers half the world, Il Maestro serving as both imperator and king. His jurisprudence is simple, robust and fair. People are still getting accustomed to such bracing air after decades of being insulated from reality under the globalist patchwork that still covers the rest of North America. But the revival of sacred kingship has struck an undoubted chord in the masses. The Curia fume, and possibly wonder how they turn Il Maestro's centralization (of sorts) to their own advantage if and when he dies.

[...]

Visited Stella again. No news of Karl, but she surprised me in her insight.

While there I couldn't help myself – I launched into a violent tirade against Whizz and his entire stinking production of *Zauberflöte*. I expressed a wish to teleport him naked to the top of Mt. Rainier during a snowstorm, then watch him run jabbering down the mountain, slowly dying of exposure.

"But why does the king want two operas premiering so close together, dad? Surely there aren't that many opera fans *left* in Seattle?"

"He's a great fan of Mozart, while the old guard Nor'westers are far more into Wagner. So it was a compromise."

"Your rivalry with Whizz is political?"

"*Political?* Haven't you been listening? It couldn't be more *personal*. I've hated that rat-faced little squelch since the first minute I ever heard him open his pale, flabbering lips."

"But why?"

"He dared to suggest my production of *La Traviata* could have used some improvements...and even had the temerity to suggest them to me!"

"Is that all? Look, I was thinking of going to *see* his production of *The Magic Flute*..."

"Don't you dare!"

"Now listen, Dad. I read a synopsis of the plot, and it sounded interesting. So perhaps you could tell me a bit about the Parsifal story...then I can decide which one I like best."

"You don't watch an opera based on the *story*," I spluttered, aghast.

"Why not?"

I looked for the words, but couldn't find them. She let me off by asking about the plot again, which I grudgingly outlined for her, and she considered a while in silence.

I was just about to leave when she sat bolt upright, entranced. It was as if a computer had taken possession of her, and she began to reel out 'hidden connections' (so she said) between the 'inner meanings' of *Parsifal* and *The Magic Flute*. I don't remember all that she said, but it was stuff along the lines of "Klingsor and his Valley of Temptation = Queen of the Night" and so forth…sometimes valid, sometimes forced comparisons. Or maybe she could see something that I couldn't.

"Parsifal has to wander, and Tamino has to find his way through the labyrinth, and Kundry is Parsifal's Pamina…"

"No, that's rubbish. Kundry is *never* the object of romantic love."

"She's not to be loved like Pamina…only compassion can do anything for *her*…in *Parsifal* it's compassion that wins, and in *The Magic Flute* it's courage and wisdom. Parsifal replaces Amfortas, and Tamino will surely succeed Sarastro…eternal renewal, the passing of the torch. As Led Zeppelin put it, the song remains the same."

"You know my opinion of rock music."

"But who do *we*, the Wolves of Joy pass *our* torch to? The emperor threatens our inner revolution. Is he in the grip of Klingsor?"

"Isn't he rather Sarastro, the wise and benevolent ruler? There's peace now…people are happier than they were before. Don't you think you're being a bit selfish?"

She frowned. She didn't know. "Power wielded too long can kill you inside," she murmured.

I didn't know what to say to that, and in any case had to leave.

[…]

My daughter may have valiantly and wisely attempted to reconcile two operas vastly different in tone, but I don't care…I will have my revenge over the costumes incident.

---

142

Whizz's prize prop, a ruined pyramid, ordered from a firm in China, and meant to be some kind of trendy 'up-to-date' (I hate that) reference to the Giza bombing…well, I had an idea about what might happen to it, based on the oft-repeated story about Wagner's dragon's head ending up in Beirut instead of Bayreuth. But aside from our now infernally unreliable international postal system, what city has a name like Seattle – Seoul? Saskatoon? Sarajevo? Anyway, the firm doubtless knows *exactly* where the opera is taking place.

Then I had another brainwave – I would get the pyramid's dimensions changed from feet to inches (like the dolmen in the old comedy *This is Spinal Tap*). I sent an email to the firm informing them as to the new measurements, but they replied shortly afterwards, confused as to why it should be changed – from metric! Damn. Whizz will probably learn of it now, and beef up his security. Fortunately, I have a trump card.

[…]

Ha! Have done it, thanks to an old acquaintance (who must remain unnamed but is currently a stagehand in Whizz's employ). I possess compromising information regarding his homosexuality (now a criminal offence), and so it was easy to get him to agree to place a specially modifed asthma pump, filled with helium, in Papageno's whistle. As it turned out, it wouldn't fit…but he managed to insert it instead into Tamino's magic flute, which turned out to be even more comically ludicrous in its effects. The audience at McCaw Hall (now renamed the Adolf Hitler Center for the Performing Arts) were reduced to tears of laughter. Even the king himself found it hard to stifle a smile, I noted with satisfaction.

Apparently Whizz has vowed revenge.
Well, let him try his best. My stick hand itches…


[…]


The king, Il Maestro, has dropped in on me personally to see how our production is going. He takes a lively interest in the arts, or so he says, especially a Gesamtkunstwerk like that we are engaged on. He is perhaps the strangest person I have met, in that I was never really sure whether I was talking to him, or to someone pretending to be him. Is he a placebo? His visage, scarred as it is, looks young, though his voice has the coolness of ancient marble, the recalling of which disconcerts me.

He mentioned the Magic Flute fiasco. I gave a dignified tut tut, not knowing if Whizz had already voiced his suspicions to him, and assured him nothing of the sort will happen with our more professional production, on which he gave a cold smile betokening aloofness from artists' jealousies and the like. Fair enough…would that we could all occupy such heightened ground. It's far too late for me, however.

I thought it best to admit of numerous small problems – not least of which being that our only decent bass-baritone has the flu – of the kind unavoidable when pulling such a complex production together, and he warmed to me more after that.

Our talk then turned to politics, and I must admit that my own problems seem insignificant compared to Il Maestro's. White people of all descriptions are now fleeing here via Canada, risking death and torture to do so, and the erstwhile 'White Republic' (now a Kingdom) has actually had to collude with Curia states in hermetically sealing its borders – to Whites! There is no alternative by reason of arable economy – this particular lifeboat is full – and yet they come…

Il Maestro pays a heavy tribute to the harsh vagaries of existence, but there is no doubt he is more tolerant and enlightened than many of his subjects, and is even attempting to revive his idea of a glass bead university, disrupted when its previous locale fell under Presidential control. And at the former Evergreen State College (now the Ezra Pound College of Liberal Arts) he has employed none other than Gallinule, that open-minded experimenter who wants greater public input on the directions of science. Gallinule's tenure was greeted with *outrage* from the Curia – disproportionately one would think – but what's that here in the real world?

We also spoke of the Wolves, and Karl – the nature of whose mission Il Maestro refused to divulge, although he confided there is a good chance he will return alive (he is now aligned to the king and not the Wolves, which must be unknown news to Stella).

From hints dropped, I believe Il Maestro's plan is to create a truly global Reich as the only way to guard against globalism – the delicious irony of which has filled me with a warmth I have lacked since the last bottle of real claret went dry. But he appears, rather interestingly, to believe himself divinely appointed (i.e. he himself is a man, but the kingship is divine), and thus seems to regard self-willed groups like the Wolves as potentially treasonous.

I pointed out how good-hearted they are (even against my own better judgement), but he went quiet, then indicated to his bodyguards that our conversation was at an end, and left, flanked by two mountainous flunkies.

[…]

145

Vicious argument between Iain, our concert master (who I know for a fact is part Jew, though I keep quiet about this as there is no proof, and it's not something he would want bandied around in the current climate) and Michael, our Gurnemanz, still recovering from flu, who really shouldn't have been in to rehearsal at all, and who is probably the most sympathetic of our crew to the new regime's ideas. And so the ancient pattern repeats.

Il Maestro now protects Jews from reprisals (in his other lands – they were officially banished from the NW, of course, long before he came on the scene) provided they don't meddle with politics or culture, or have any contact with their brethren in the Curia lands or in Israel (which although not governed by the Curia, is militarily aligned with it, or something like that). Of course, Jews in Curia lands shriek that even *this* is persecution, spreading rumours Il Maestro is committing 'anti-Semitic atrocities', including some rather hideous medical experiments...conversely, however, in the North West, there have been mutterings he is a 'Jew-lover'.

Iain and Michael, who both have to be careful what they say in public, were berating each other over minor details of Il Maestro's attitude to Israel, but there were deeper, unspoken issues at stake, which made it fascinating to watch (in a sadistic kind of way). Part of their argument related to Israel's sudden courting of non-Curia ethnostates. Only a decade ago it was quite common for nationalist parties in the West to express solidarity with Israel, even though the latter only ever repaid their solicitations with contempt. When the NW Republic was first established, its leaders vowed never to repeat such obvious stupidity, choosing to ignore Israel completely.

But the Israeli Right has suddenly changed its tune,

making cautious overtures to a handful of non-Curia-approved ethnostates in the Imperium (apparently behind the Curia's back). There is a sense in Israel (among non-hardliners) that the Zionist project is winding down, as the Curia itself abandons its child, despite the former being originally founded by Bilderberg types as a more pro-Israel version of the UN.

Our concert master insists that this newfound regard for other ethnostates on Israel's part is something genuine, while our bass-baritone gloats that it is too little too late, and that the "shitty little country" deserves to die, frozen and friendless.

At the same time, Il Maestro's more relaxed attitude to Jews has created tensions in his own lands, leading to rumours that he covets their money-making skills. This has added to the tensions already present in many of his dominions, where tribalism leads the people to chafe at the very notion of Imperium, and indeed the idea of peace in general. It is unclear how long one man's (admittedly forceful) persona will be able to hold it all together.

Meanwhile, here in the Northwest, someone is writing an epic poem, reviving the form, and our Gurnemanz loves this idea. But my daughter and her friends seem to think the 'neo-troubadours' of Il Maestro's court (modelled on themselves) lack sincerity, having form only. You can't please everyone…

I have heard other, more worrying rumours, too – that Il Maestro wishes to turn away from the world and probe the deepest mysteries of physics and mathematics, and would do so were it not for small matters constantly engaging him, wearing him down. But if he abdicates, what hope for the civilized?

[…]

Sleepless in Seattle. I wandered the streets for hours, hand aclench my firm and cherished stick. The city is so soulless at night…the revolution hasn't gone far enough, as the sense of prim nothingness in certain quarters is still undiminished. At times like this I feel like a dissenter, a dissenter from eveything. Not a rebel though…never a rebel.

Some oldster moaning about 'chemtrails' asks me for a dollar, still legal tender in the royal domains, increasingly rare in rural regions, and I give it him to shut him up. The incident seems completely void of sense and depth. Then I pass a so-called 'eccentric' called Dr. Moon, sitting on a front stoop teaching invented languages to a decaying leaf. That, too, lacks depth and sense.

This kingdom we inhabit – how long will it last, when all the civilizations of history have eventually ended? Ours hasn't even created a unique culture of its own – just rehashing Mozart and Wagner. But again, give it time. It may find its feet after I am gone. That is a sacrifice I would gladly make. History is unforgiving…

And tonight I passed the exact place, Tinders, where I first met my wife. And felt nothing. Everything is turning to plastic. What's wrong with me?

Faces flash in front of me – Chugg and his friends who bullied me in Middle School before I learnt to fight back. Are *they* out there in this plastic city, or did they flee to the Presidential States? So distant…all so long ago. Bullies amuse me now. I'm getting old, and there is little that scares me, not with treasured stick at hand. I swished it at a fence, where faded spraypaint proclaimed that 'Kurt lives', and smiled wryly. I well remember the Cobain killing (suicide it was called at the time), which happened when I was thirteen. Even back then I hated rock 'n' roll (except for Spinal Tap), preferring the purity of early music. So here I am doing Wagner, almost its antithesis. And yet, Wagner has a strange purity of his own when all is said and done. Mozart has his moments, too. But I want revenge…

What else did I observe tonight? Oh, yes. Two young men bullying a third youth who appeared to be simple or perhaps autistic. That sort of thing will always go on, whatever regime we live under. I contemplated interference, and eventually decided to crack one of them upside the head, whereupon both immediately fled. Not bad for a fifty-something. Their quarry shuffled off, too, regarding me with fear. I returned home to find my wayward wife there again, but this time felt no desire, nothing.

She had news – that Karl had reappeared, that he and Stella joyfully plan to marry. I wish I could get excited. Karl's mission was successful (he can't reveal the details), and Il Maestro is now considering him as a possible adoptive heir.

I acted happy and such, but feel increasingly dead inside. Maybe that's why good things are happening, and will perhaps continue to happen – because I feel dead inside. I remember the old MGTOW ('Men Going Their Own Way') movement, sometime around 2015. It was only when they turned their backs completely on women that women started *following them devotedly*, and that's how these things work.

[…]

The big night. Career on the line. King watching, world watching, so it felt. Our bass-baritone recovered marvellously, but that turned out to be the least of my worries. The dive bombers started to circle even before the curtain went up, when we discovered that the water for the lake from Act I had been adulterated with a bright, neon-pink foaming agent. Now I knew for sure that Whizz had procured an inside agent, just as I had managed to do. But who? Hubert, our fat stage manager? Trevor, who was always a bit sleazy? Surely not our esteemed concert master? There was no way of knowing, short of torturing them all.

I had them quickly drain it, making do with a dry lake. Hopefully someone in the audience might read obscure mystical symbolism into that, or something. Then I had the stagehands doublecheck everything, working in pairs in case one of them should be the traitor. I wanted to retreat to my nest, my shell, but it wasn't possible. I scoured the opera house for Whizz (or anyone recognizable as having associated with him), but nothing, just a mess of strange faces splurging out at me.

This double checking was in vain, anyway, as we found at the end of Act I, in the realm where time becomes space, when the mist grew steadily worse. The dry ice machine had been tampered with, creating an impenetrable fog which enveloped the audience, king and all. It was all too much for my poor little head.

To my immense surprise, however, the applause at the end of the Act (contra tradition, I know, but I'm not a Wagnerian) was *warm*. Incredibly, we had gotten away with it, Whizz's sabotage merely *adding* to the audience's experience of the timeless realm of the Grail!

But then came the next act, and at a certain point my brain clicked into gear (I shudder to recall), noticing layered echoes of snickers like ancient starter motors, building incrementally, but it was some time before I worked out what they were snickering *at* – namely, that our esteemed Klingsor had a problem south of the border (I later learned his drink had been spiked with Ellison

Plugg's brand of super-strength erectile formula), and that his tights would consequently need replacing. (Our servicable soprano Ellen, playing Kundry, is unentrancing to look upon, so small wonder, perhaps, that there were snickers.)

Then I spotted him, Whizz, in the second row of the audience, evidently placed so as to get a good view (the acoustics are terrible there). The smug smirk on his face told me everything. I marched up intending to shirtfront him, and beat him with my stick, caring no whit if the king were looking or not (he was), but was preempted somewhat when, grinning inanely, he threw the contents of his wine glass with some vigor into my face. A brawl ensued, not unlike that in a Beatrix Potter story about a fox and badger whose name escapes me, and to my great pride (at the time) and utter disbelief (now) the greater part of the cast joined in, for Whizz was surrounded by a dozen laughing cronies on either side. Several art lovers, who had the misfortune to be stationed in the front row, were enmeshed unwillingly in the brawl, as the orchestra stopped playing, and female screams rebounded. To cut a long story short, Act III was cancelled and Il Maestro was unamused.

And now I have been summonsed for instigating, and for violation of parole – and while my soon-to-be son-in-law will probably get me off, is it really worth the constant degrading lectures from my daughter on "White people fighting over factional trivialities…our undoing as a people"?

Oh yes…I was acting out the age-old drama all right.

I don't care, though. I got him a good one, with the most exquisite stick in the world.

## 10

## THE TESTIMONY OF
## MAXINE LEOPOLDINA SCARLOTTI

My dreams are all of fire – mother says dreams usually go by opposites, so does that mean the world will end in ice? With my father listening to his underlings so much, to sly people like Mr. Adam Bray, it would not surprise me if the world ended in ice...

Mother says the only neutral state, Russia, was recaptured by the Curia on the death of the ancient Putin ("whose motives were impeccable, whose methods were questionable", she said, or was it the other way around?), and now the wizened Curia vultures threaten father's Imperium once again. In response, he stops treating his subject states kindly, and works towards a military superstate for some "looming last battle".

And now, even as he finally lets me take his surname as my own, he pressures me to enter into a betrothal contract with the vile Enzo, a sort of hired killer! I told father I would rather join the Wolves, and his eyes blazed in rage. When he calmed down, he told me to "think on it", but his tone indicated he would brook no opposition, and that my 'choice' was not a free one. So, I am resolved to run away.

They say father has actually begun to persecute the Wolves. The legendary outlaw Sean was assassinated in a place called Risdon Prison, and no one has admitted to ordering the killing. At the same time, father passes laws against 'anti-semitism', and although this is aimed only at stopping criminal attacks, it has alienated many of his followers, who think it is the thin end of the wedge for a "revival of Zionist values", or something. It's all very complicated and sad.

Father also says he wants Israel left alone (when even its own citizens are starting to abandon it en masse), because he doesn't want them infesting the West with their 'endless victim swindle' – he wants to use Israel as a stopgap until he can implement something called the 'Birobidjan solution', but apparently this will be extremely difficult now that Russia is back in Curia hands.

And now he is launching a massive military expedition against the 'Bloc' (Eastern Europe, that is, not counting Russia), and the Curia are giving him less opposition than expected, because it's more of a *genuine* independence movement (from both Curia and father) that he's suppressing.

And *I* am going to defy him, the most powerful man in the world, and can only imagine two outcomes – death or imprisonment on one hand, or a tearful reunion, with father agreeing to make an 'official' version of the Wolves, although the Wolves themselves will think it is corrupt and refuse to join. But as I'm not exactly the apple of my father's eye, I think the first outcome is more likely anyway.

How dark and tangled everything has become!

Surely it never started out like this…

## 11

## THE TESTIMONY OF
## WALLACE TARR

I give this brief rememberance of His Imperial Majesty, Maximillian I. While not a literary man, I will try and paint a picture of His Imperial Majesty as he was in his last days.

My most distinct memory is standing alongside him for nearly an hour as he appeared to contemplate the landscape from where we stood – a barren hill on the edge of the Gobi Desert where a wide belt of green grassland met a neverending sea of brown and sterile sandhills. When he finally moved his noble head, it was to gaze upwards at a flock of overlanding birds flying high above. One of us, Hubert I think, found courage to speak, saying something to the effect that the birds were probably fleeing a distant storm.

And then, in the far beyond, we finally spied the men we were waiting for, changing from motes to full stops and then standing still, hundreds of them, as if contemplating us from remote antiquity. You could almost see their necks craning to assess us, and then, swiftly and silently, they turned and galloped away...just as I had expected, and probably the others too, because nobody raised a murmur. These kinds of traitors, who saw only the immediate needs of their tribe rather than the greater struggle...yes, we were well adapted to their sort.

It had recently looked like coming rain (something

which apparently never happened at this time of year) but now the clouds seemed to be moving backwards, as if a vast mouth were sucking clean the sky, each cloud detached from the others, shivering and lonely, yet ingested by the same force, so their loneliness mattered not at the end…yet one couldn't feel glad for them. More than one of us had the strange feeling that the sun would not continue to rise over this desert for very much longer.

The emperor, responding to this familiar situation, voiced his opinion that *time never repeats*, and that a theory called 'Eternal Return' is wrong, that patterns really reform slightly different each time, similar but never exact.

"The prison walls which some allege precisely defined, are in fact eternal and therefore impregnable," he stated. "Therefore we should be content with shoring up those walls, like Gilgamesh did at the end of his great adventure."

I vowed to read the story of this Gilgamesh so I could better understand what he was talking about – but one doesn't interrupt the emperor with questions when he is waxing philosophical.

Unexpectedly, though, Hans (who though timid and shy has always seemed a loyal and devoted servant of His Imperial Majesty, at least to myself) did something completely out of character. He not only interrupted the Emperor, but took him to task, speaking in a tremulous voice of prophecy, saying that: "Like Théoden of legend, you need a Gandalf the White to open your eyes, *then* you will find the walls to be pregnable. And the Wolves will return…"

But the Emperor sent him away in a fury, uttering these words:

"I love everything that has ever existed, even my nefarious enemies, so am I not Master of all, never to be defied? What need of breaching walls, when walls are *loved?* Would not breaching them be an act of hatred and malice? Would I not then cease to be Master, and become a nefarious enemy of life itself in my own right?"

And no one could answer these words of His Imperial Majesty.

Then news came in by radio, seeming to kill the moon, which we only then realised we couldn't locate in the sky, although it was supposed to be an Evening Moon. *[He means a waxing one, presumably – E.J.C.].* There had been a nuclear attack by terrorists, though no one was sure who they actually were, somewhere in the wastes of Central Asia – not so very far from where we stood (and so why couldn't we hear the presumably vast report – had the moon sucked it up, and hence been temporarily displaced?).

His Imperial Majesty was aching to hit the trail towards our next battle, but wisely decided to wait for further reports before moving out. These reports, which seemed far-off and near all at once, could be irrelevant or a deadly trap…it seemed impossible to tell which. All we knew for sure was that the situation in camp was very tense, and when at a certain moment I felt drops of rain on my upturned face my first guess was that they were a spray of tears shaken from somebody's head in the darkening congress.

It was just as well that we waited, for over the next week, the news trickled in – a disease, spreading rapidly, which we now know as the Grey Death, its lines of advance largely to the westwards and seemingly avoiding us, but not by much…like the blade of a scythe, hovering for a killing blow that never quite landed, yet making us fear the open skies themselves.

It was reckoned that the nuclear blast had encompassed the site of an ancient kurgan, from which bacteria had escaped that the explosion itself hadn't managed to kill.

So who carried out the attack, and why? Did it matter? Did he who knew have mysterious permission to pass on beyond the plane of bacteria and suchlike obfuscations? The Grey Death, they call it, but in colour-change it is opposite to Gandalf – for where he had turned from grey to white, the disease started out in the latter state…for when slapping the skin of an aflictee with a specialised spatula with a hole in its centre, a small white pustule invariably appears, and then, a few days later, the body equally invariably becomes grey and brittle, dying from within, a coral polyp making the unimagined transition to dried sea sponge, without anyone knowing or caring, or waiting in the wings.

So many 'outbreaks' in the past (swine flu etc.), hyped by vaccine companies to make a quick buck, but this time it was actually real, and horrific, and there wasn't a thing anyone could do about it, not even an explanation. Sickness, dissipation, hallmarks of the Piscean Age, and we are now living in its last gasp, made plaintive solely by intensity, one final wring of the cloth, squeezing out all the concentrated diseased dregs, so that one might say it is the very spirit of disease, while all the time a new world is attempting to be born.

And under the cloth itself, countless lives swirled, stripped to their essence, pared to the Archetype, which no matter how the opposition protest, keeps pushing back. Without it, we would *all* be nothing but grey and brittle sea sponges, and the universe itself would be chalk dust, which no one would see – so in truth wouldn't exist.

And probably just as well this Archetype primes me, sending dreams, which then translate to action. In one, a dry sea sponge embraces a wet fish, both turning to sludge, which is then stored in an exquisite cup, fit for His Imperial Majesty to drink from (if he didn't choose to drink as he does from ordinary vessels).

And when I awoke from this dream, I heard the first

report on the final implosion of the 'Smash the Archetype' movement, which had lately spread through the entire world…

The moment of collapse did not come during the long slow weeks when the painful realisation came to these narcissists that they themselves were an archetype. No, it came later – when they realised that they were *a low one*. The pitiful remainder of the once mighty movement can now be witnessed begging for penance, from beggars, on many a street corner throughout the world.

And then I thought of my betrothed, Elanna, whom I will never see again on this side of the curtain. (Already the disease toll exceeds that of the Black Death of the 1340s, and is wider in scope, thanks to jet travel.) And I thought of her warmth, her physical presence, wondering if it was an illusion or whether it had been real. I never realised how good she was until now that she is once more unattainable.

Pity me not, though, for I die among warriors.

Then, after a seeming eternity, the emperor gave the order to move out, for if our troops were affected, then so would the enemy's be. And never was army more ready – we were "harder than Krupp steel," as the saying goes, and fought like men possessed, against a numerically even army which had no chance. Hail Caesar, those who are about to die salute you! It was the emperor's final *human* act – though not his final endeavour. I remember the frenzy as if it were now upon me, albeit felt via another person, an opium penance. I remember the very last time I caught His Imperial Majesty's eye, as we wiped the blood from our skin, panting in confused contamination, staring at a world grown distant and plastic. Whence would new blood flow, giving nearness and depth?

But above all I remember the morning after combat, when I awoke at dawn to see His Imperial Majesty standing still and staring up at the sky, like a prophet of old searching for a silent warning. Then he turned and loped swiftly like a wolf to his campaign tent.

What he had seen, I later learned, was a vision of the Morning Star, whose cold, serene yet steely light seemed to bathe his face even hours later when he addressed us on the matter.

He had found, he said, an old testimony in his campaign bag, which he now intended to make public, having read it for the first time since it was written. First, though, he read from it the record of a dream, in which he had torn and gouged his own skin…reading this, he said, had made him realise that he was *not* a reincarnation of Pyrrhus of Epirus as he had once claimed, but rather of one *Friedrich II von Hohenstaufen*, a medieval German ruler.

"How did I not see it before?" he pondered, realising now that the dream about Pyrrhus had in actuality been someone else *telling* him (i.e. Friedrich II) about Pyrrhus. He was also clear that this past life heritage had caused him to emulate, in various ways, the life of Friedrich II.

But Hans, who had found the courage to return, or perhaps couldn't keep away from the chieftain he both loved and chastised, leapt onto the podium and began to debate with His Imperial Majesty on the nature of reality, reincarnation and the rest of it.

This time, though, and I know not how it happened, their arguments were *reversed*…this time it was Hans who argued that the analogies His Imperial Majesty thought he had found between his own life and that of Friedrich II were not exact, that history doesn't repeat, it merely rhymes, and that the rhymes themselves are irregular, more like blank verse really, and that life is an infinitely-changing fractal, with no exact Eternal Return etc.

And now His Imperial Majesty argued that it was Hans who needed a *Gandalf the White* to awaken him from

159

his slumber, yet closing with mysterious words, said: "I will atone for what I did in that other existence..."

And next day he was gone...disappeared in the deep night, like a seeping shadow. It was a week before we learnt what actually happened. And some have speculated that, having made public and left behind the journal (which he had instructed wasn't to be made public before his death) he now had no choice but to die as a result.

In any case, all the world now knows how he arrived for an unscheduled truce meeting with the executive council of the Unicursal Curia and, using technology he had sponsored or developed himself (and which has still not been made public) caused their heads to literally explode, dying a foreseen death himself in the process (for, of course, his own head exploded along with theirs).

And on his body was found a card with these two quotes:

"He who manages to bind the golem and refine him
will be reconciled with himself."
– Meyrink

"At the end of the play, something occurs that its
creators never envisaged...life always finds a way, and
that is what these Curia types will never understand..."
– Scarlotti

On the back of the card was a single word: "Tegg."

So while a green new world may well emerge from the shadow of the old, I will not myself be here to see it, for the sickness is upon me, and my grey phase begins – already I feel my bones turn brittle.

But I have had the privilege of knowing one of history's greatest lords, and nothing can take that away from me.

Hail Caesar, for those who are about to die salute you!

## AFTERWORD

Now that you have perused the material, ending with that terrible massacre of the Inner Council, keep in mind the near certainty that Scarlotti's story of the guru's cave was *invented*, perhaps a safe way of explaining inner impulses he didn't understand, as no such cave was found within a forty mile radius of Sterns, and nor was any student with the name or nickname of Tegg ever enrolled there.

On further investigation, it appears that 'Maximillian Scarlotti' was not even his real name, and that no one knows how he got into Sterns in the first place, the records of his enrolment process having been found non-existent.

Consequently, we *Weltverbesserer* would now be wise to shift our attention to the planet Venus herself, and when we gain the upper hand once more, to form, from existing warheads, a vast nuclear armada to tear her baleful presence from the shivering skies.

- Elmer J. Cohen
(former) Special Advisor to the
(former) Unicursal Curia

*By the same author*

**The Hungry Wolves of Van Diemen's Land**
(2014)

"*The Hungry Wolves of Van Diemen's Land* is the first book I would lend to someone who wanted to understand those who eschew the hypocritical Zeitgeist of the baby boom generation. Anyone who is questioning the system's narratives relating to history, to current events and to the "inevitable" future that the system would like to put in place. Anyone on the brink of awakening..."

- Juleigh Howard-Hobson, author of *"I do not belong to the Baader-Meinhof Group" and Other Poems*

Made in the USA
Middletown, DE
25 November 2015